M000073547

# CONTENTS

## ANNIHILATION

## BOOKS IN THE FORSAKEN MERCENARY UNIVERSE

### FORSAKEN MERCENARY CASE FILES

# STAY INFORMED

Get A Free Book by visiting Jonathan Yanez' website. You can email me at jonathan.alan.yanez@gmail.com or find me on Amazon, and Instagram (@author_jonathan_yanez). I also created a special Facebook group called "Jonathan's Reading Wolves" specifically for readers, where I show new cover art, do giveaways, and run contests. Please check it out and join whenever you get the chance!

For updates about new releases, as well as exclusive promotions, visit my website and sign up for the VIP mailing list. Head there now to receive free stories.

*www.jonathan-yanez.com*

Enjoying the series? Help others discover *Forsaken Mercenary* by sharing with a friend.

# ANNIHILATION

FORSAKEN MERCENARY BOOK FIVE

# ONE

ONE DAY UNTIL VOY INVASION

THERE WAS a reason I didn't watch the news or go on one of the dozens of social media platforms available to the average consumer. When the Voy broadcasted their presence to humankind, I was reminded of this.

As you can probably imagine, every news station and social media platform went wild with the emergence of our new alien friends. Within hours, there were reports of rioting on the moon and general unrest on Mars.

Earth was mostly taken out of the equation. There weren't many people left on it and they weren't important to those in power.

"Things on Mars are about to boil over," X informed me as she scrolled through dozens of reports coming through to us via our new Galactic Government allies. She showed me these graphs and bullet points in a small screen that popped up in the lower right corner of my vision. "It's about to get as bad here as it is on the moon."

X ran through a few images of the events on the moon. Densely populated, the cities of the moon were primed for an event like this. Mobs hit the streets. There were people chanting and holding signs that read, "They are not our enemy, you are" and "Stop killing innocent aliens."

It was clear these people had no idea what was really going on. It was a brilliant move by the Voy to release a statement to humanity showing inaccurate footage of dead Voy. They made it look as if they were innocent, doing nothing more than extending an olive branch and we slaughtered them. Nothing could be further from the truth.

The truth was the Voy ambushed the GG and we saved our Galactic Government counterparts. But that truth was dead, now smeared by the insanity of mob mentality.

I waited along with X and Butch in the garage of Dragon Hold. Cassie promised some kind of weapon that would give us a fighting chance against the Voy horde when they attacked.

I wasn't positive what the weapon was, but I was willing to go with her and get it. The plan was for a small group of us to head into Athens, secure whatever it was Cassie needed, and head back.

Butch sauntered over to the various vehicles in the garage, giving them a good sniffing. She sneezed a few times as she huffed in the scents of oil and gasoline.

"Bless you," I told the animal.

I relished the smell myself. There was something calming about the scent of metal and oil. These were things that made sense. These were machines that played by a specific set of rules in a world full of aliens, and dare I say it, magic.

One second, I was lost in my own thoughts; the next second, Madam Eternal stood right next to me.

"Holy—" I stopped there, one hand already on the handle of my MK II. "You can't be sneaking up on people like that. I almost shot you."

"I apologize," Madam Eternal said with a deep smile. "I didn't mean to frighten you."

Butch stalked over to my side, her head low, her eyes on the woman. A deep, menacing growl came from the giant wolf.

"Peace, sister." Madam Eternal showed both her palms, open and free of malice. "We are allies in this, not enemies."

Butch didn't look like she trusted her any more than she did before Madam Eternal spoke, but at least she stopped growling.

Madam Eternal stood there a moment, holding the animal's eye. The leader of her own corporation, Madam Eternal was known for dealing in medicines

and healing arts. There were those among the corporations that deemed her abilities magical and not science.
Others were content to turn a blind eye to her doings
as long as she was on their side.

She was an older woman, fit and beautiful with long
hair down her back. She smiled easily and had a way of
speaking that made you feel as though you'd known
her longer than you actually had.

I for one didn't care if she was stirring a boiling pot
of potion in her room. We had a job to do. The Voy
needed to die. If she was onboard with that, then she
was okay by me.

"I was wondering if you might make a slight detour
on your way to pick up The Order's supplies," Madam
Eternal asked. "It wouldn't take you more than a few
kilometers out of the way. And I can assure you that it
is paramount to our success against the Voy during
tomorrow's battle."

"What is it?" I asked. My first thought was to tell
her no, but I was willing to hear her out.

"I can't tell you that because you wouldn't believe
me nor might you understand," Madam Eternal said
with one of her easy smiles. "I can tell you that it will
give us an edge against the Voy. It could mean turning
the tide of war."

"Try me," I told her. "You may be surprised what
I'm willing to believe. I've seen a lot of messed-up stuff
lately."

"There is a device to summon aid that will be able to assist us against the Voy when they attack," Madam Eternal stated simply. "I cannot guarantee that with it we will win, but I can guarantee it will be of great help."

"Device? Summon? Aid?" I asked all three questions, halting between each one.

"I told you that you wouldn't believe me." Madam Eternal shrugged. "Some things you just have to take on faith. I'll send the coordinates to your AI as soon as I re-enter the Hold."

"I'm—"

I was going to say a lot more and question the woman further, when the door to the garage opened from inside the Hold. Echo and Samantha walked out along with Cassie.

"We ready to roll?" Cassie asked.

"Yeah, we'll take Butch with us on this one," I said, nodding toward what looked like a large armored truck. "I think that's the vehicle we want."

"I'll drive," Echo said, practically jumping toward the vehicle. He had just been released from his cell minutes before, but it was clear Echo was eager to show us he meant to keep his word.

Sam and Cassie followed.

I looked back to address Madam Eternal. The woman was gone.

"How does she do that?" I muttered to myself.

Butch and I followed the others to the armored truck. The vehicle was a beast with a reinforced steel grill mounted to the front. Heavy-duty tires rolled the metal monster forward and steel plating attached to the sides.

"I'll ride shotgun," Cassie said, opening up the passenger side door and climbing inside.

Sam and I made for the back, where two rear doors opened up to reveal a pair of bench seats facing each other in a box-like compartment at the rear of the truck.

Sam hopped inside, folding the top section and bottom section of her bow. The weapon wasn't more than a meter wide now and easier for her to carry.

Butch jumped in without hesitation. I followed and shut the doors, taking a seat across from Sam.

Echo gunned the engine. The vehicle roared to life, vibrating as the noise filled the inside of the garage.

"We have a detour to make along the way," I said, making the split second decision there and then to run Madam Eternal's little errand for her. The hard facts were we could use any help we could get against the Voy. Madam Eternal, for all her cryptic ways, hadn't led us astray yet.

"Little detour?" Sam arched an eyebrow in front of me. "This isn't the time for a snack run."

"Not a snack run, but that doesn't sound half bad," I said, thinking back to the last time I had eaten. Had breakfast really been so recent? "X, can you send the coordinates Madam Eternal gave you to Echo and Cassie?"

"Done," X answered out loud.

"What does Madam Eternal want us to get?" Cassie said, opening the holo display on the back of her left robotic forearm. "Why can't she get it herself?"

"You know her better than I do," I answered to the back of Cassie's head. "She said she has something that will help us battle the Voy. That's enough for me."

"You're the boss," Cassie said with a shrug.

Echo moved the armored truck out of the garage and rolled down the sand-covered driveway of Dragon Hold. The area in front of the mansion was teeming with many factions of people from Way followers to corporation mercenaries. It was a wonder they could work side by side.

The only way that was possible was because of the Voy. In the face of a mutual threat, it was truly amazing what could be accomplished.

A long blaster-proof window rested above each of the benches along the wall, offering us a view.

I looked past Sam then at her.

"Yes?" the redhead asked. "Do I have something on my face?"

"Nope, you just shouldn't be here," I said above the roar of the armored truck. "You should go back."

"Excuse me?" Sam asked.

"You heard me," I answered, thinking about Amber and the baby in her belly that wasn't mine. "You have a family, you were out. No one here is going to judge you if you go back."

"Family isn't just decided by blood," Sam said, looking actually pissed I'd even bring up the subject. "I go where I want. I stand with whom I choose. My husband and daughter understand that. I wouldn't be the person they've grown to love if I turned my back on the world now when it needs me the most."

Butch had taken up a position in the space between us. She lay down panting, looking at both Sam and me. The tone in Sam's voice caused Butch to lower her snout and look at me with those big yellow eyes of hers as if to say, "You've really pissed her off now."

"I'm glad you're here," I said, sinking into my seat as Echo exited the heavy gates of the grounds and turned onto the street. "I just want you to know that."

The pissed-off look in Sam's eyes evaporated. She nodded toward me then jerked her chin upward, changing the subject.

"So you're the Master of Dragon Hold, leader of Immortal Corp, and head of the corporations fighting against the Voy? How much has happened since I saw you back on Earth?" Sam asked, half amused, half stunned. "You get around."

"One day I need to put it all in a book," I said,

letting a long puff of air blow past my lips. "I guess I can give you the short version now."

I told Sam everything that had happened since I last saw her, including getting captured by the Voy, inheriting Dragon Hold, and rescuing the GG.

Sam's jaw dropped open further and further as my story continued.

"Then I threw my axe into the mouth of the oversized bug and gave it a headache you wouldn't believe," I ended the story. "I still kind of smell from all the blood and guts that coated me."

"That's disgusting," Sam said with a grimace.

"Yeah, you're telling me," I answered. "I was cleaning the stuff out of every ho—"

"Sorry to interrupt your autobiography, but we've got trouble," Cassie said from her seat in the passenger side of the armored truck. "You should take a look at this."

Even though her warning was very serious, there was a calm in her voice that said we'd find a way to get past whatever it was.

I stood and crouched to look past her shoulder out the windshield in front of us. We were in a section of Athens I hadn't visited before. Corporate buildings rose high on either side of the wide street.

A heavy GG presence ahead of us punctuated Cassie's words. Along with the GG was a mob of panicked Athens citizens shouting and ready to riot.

# TWO

I WAS STUNNED there were even this many people in Athens. The city made up of only the richest of the rich had at most times been a ghost town. It seemed those with wealth didn't need to leave their villas or penthouses much.

The other bad thing was that these people were wealthy enough to have their own bodyguards and security teams. I could pick out dozens of armed men and women in the crowd.

"Why didn't we just take a dropship to run these errands?" Echo asked.

"All were being used to transport equipment and people to the staging ground outside the city," Cassie said under her breath. "How did all these people get out here so fast? It couldn't be more than a few hours since the Voy message broadcasted."

"Fear does strange things to people," Sam said next to me as she too craned her neck forward to get a better view of what was about to happen.

"Please go back to your homes!" a Galactic Government praetorian instructed via a speaker mounted inside his helmet. "You need to disperse immediately."

I couldn't pick out which of the praetorians in front of us was on the horn. There had to be close to a hundred of the mustard-armored praetorians blocking the street with their heavy assault vehicles.

"We understand this is a confusing time right now," the praetorian continued. "Please go back to your homes. We'll have further information for you as soon as we know more."

Echo had the windows rolled down so we could hear all the shouting in return to the praetorian's commands.

I had no doubt in my mind this wasn't going to end well. The wealthy were used to getting their way.

The mob was too far away and there were too many of them screaming to pick out full phrases, but I heard things like:

"The docking port is packed."

"Can't get off Mars."

"End times."

"Why aren't more of them trying to get out of the city?" I asked anyone who would have an answer. "I mean, don't all their vehicles have the ability to fly? If they can't get off Mars in their vehicles, then maybe they can at least leave the city and create some distance between them and the Voy."

"The Galactic Government has locked down all vehicles on Mars that are able to fly," X answered out loud so everyone could hear. "In moments of crises such as this, the government has had inhibitors implanted in vehicles to keep them on the ground. The idea being that in instances of great distress, citizens would take to the air in the hover vehicles, thus increasing the chances of an accident by tenfold as opposed to staying on the ground."

"Great idea," Echo muttered to himself. "And a great way to piss off thousands of people."

"The space ports on Mars are pictures of chaos as everyone is trying to leave at once," X continued. "The dropships leaving and coming from Mars are being overrun. Those rich enough to have their own ships are growing impatient waiting for the green light to depart."

"Nothing changes for us," I said, reeling the group back to the here and now. "We get the item Madam Eternal sent us to get along with the tech from the Order and we head back, end of story."

"I'm with you, but without flight, there's no way around but through," Cassie said, looking at a map of the area holo projected above her left forearm. "We can try to go through here now or around somewhere, but we'll have to get past the mob sooner or later."

"She's right," X chimed in. "We should try and enter the area here under the support of the Galactic Government. Once we're through, we'll be on our own, though. The GG has pulled resources to the city here and the surrounding space ports. They're spread thin."

"We go through here, then," I said, motioning with my chin for Echo to pull forward.

We were the only vehicle on this side of the GG line. No one wanted to go deeper into the city; they wanted to get out. Those unable to flee or burned with the misinformed idea that we should be befriending the Voy had come here to the downtown district to field their complaint.

A squad of heavily armored praetorians waved us to the side of the street. Echo complied, killing the engine.

As far as I knew, we were absolved of any crimes committed against the GG since we saved their butts back at the Way settlement. Stranger things had happened, though. I kept my right hand away from the MK II at my hip, but I knew I could draw it at a moment's notice.

Echo rolled down the window as our vehicle was surrounded.

"You need to clear off the road," the praetorian said

through his helmet. "Go stay inside your houses until you receive further orders."

"We're a private organization working with the GG," I said with what I hoped was a reassuring smile. "You can contact Captain Zoe Valentine or Colonel Jonah Strife if you need to confirm our story. We need to get through here."

The praetorian looked at us for a second longer as if he were actually seeing us for the first time.

"Hold here," he said, taking a few steps away.

I couldn't hear him past the shouting and chanting of the mob a block in front of us, but I could tell he was speaking with someone on his own comm line.

The other praetorians around our vehicle clenched their weapons tighter. I got it. We were all stressed in a scenario poised to explode. I didn't blame them for being a bit jumpy.

The praetorian we spoke with a moment before returned to the side of the armored truck.

"I'm sorry, sir, I had no idea who you and your party were, sir." The praetorian seemed flustered. "I just wanted to personally thank you and your team. I don't have all the details, but you helped my sister out of a tight spot yesterday at a Way settlement."

The praise took me off guard.

"I'm, uh—I'm glad she got out safe," I answered.

"We'll let you through, but I just want to warn you that you're going into a part of the city not patrolled by any GG units," he continued. "It might be dangerous out there."

"I think we'll take our chances," Cassie chimed in.

"Understood, ma'am." The praetorian shouted a few orders and the soldiers surrounding our vehicle moved away to inspect the next car in a line of vehicles behind us.

I hadn't noticed while we were talking, but since we had been there, a short line of people trying to maneuver through the city had piled to the rear of our armored truck.

"So weird to hear people call you 'sir,'" Sam breathed as Echo inched forward. "We used to call you a lot of things, but 'sir' was never one of them."

Echo chuckled.

"I guess a lot has changed," I said. "Careful; I'll have *you* start calling me 'sir' in a minute."

Sam rolled her eyes.

It was just our luck, as we inched toward the GG line, that was the moment all hell decided to break loose.

Weapons fire punctured the air. Yelling and screaming followed as a few wealthy individuals with their own security teams ordered their men to fire on the praetorian lines.

Who knows if it was that or maybe some trigger happy elite fancied themself an anarchist at heart and decided to light a fuse on the party.

People were mowed down in the street as everyone with a weapon exchanged fire.

Rounds pinged off and scorched the armored truck we were in.

Butch whined.

"Stomp on it!" Sam yelled.

Echo didn't need to be told twice. He hit the gas, shooting us forward into the street in front of us, blaring his horn and cursing for people to get out of the way.

Not that anyone outside the truck could hear him, but Echo had to win some kind of award for the number of inventive curse words he put together in a single string.

Sam and I grabbed the backs of the seats in front of us. We bent our knees to not get thrown to the rear. Butch stayed low and anchored.

The GG moved out of the way, finding their own cover behind vehicles and around buildings as the enemy on the opposite side did the same. Bystanders ran from the middle of the street, trying to find whatever cover the business structures on either side afforded.

Echo kept on his horn and sped forward, swerving to miss people.

As the only moving vehicle on the street, we were a magnet for rounds. The truck we were in was a tank, but everything had its limit.

Just when I thought we were going to make it out alive, we screamed through the road into an intersection and were T-boned by something massive coming down the street.

I must have cracked my head on something because I blacked out for a few seconds. I knew the armored truck was on its side. My left leg was numb with pain. I didn't remember the truck rolling, but I knew we landed on our left side, skidding down the street.

I coughed, trying to find my voice at the same time searching to find where everyone else had landed around me.

"Daniel, Daniel, are you okay?" Cassie coughed from the front passenger side seat.

Butch whined.

"Yeah, I—"

Shouting from outside cut us off as dark-clad figures surrounded our overturned vehicle. Whoever they were, they weren't part of the GG.

"We've got company," I said, looking toward Sam, who was slumped on the ground beside me. A thick line of blood that started at her hairline fell down her face. "Sam's out."

"What—what happened?" Echo asked, coming to.

"Doors, clear!" voices from outside yelled.

A pair of explosions sent a concussive wave into the interior of the vehicle.

The rear of the armored truck was blown open as

well as the passenger door next to Cassie that was now pointed to the sky.

Figures appeared out of the smoke. I drew my MK II, still fighting off the effects of a concussion as I lit into them. I took at least three out with rounds to the head. Their helmets at this close range stood no chance against the hand cannon I wielded.

I could hear Cassie and Echo behind me firing at anyone stupid enough to try and grab them via the open passenger side door.

"Gas, gas!" those outside yelled.

I knew then my only way out was through. Butch barked fiercely from her spot next to me.

"We've got to get out of here!" Cassie warned.

"Go!" I answered. "I've got Sam."

"Cover me. I can get her," Echo said, crawling over to the woman and lifting her over his wide shoulders.

There was no time to argue. Gas canisters were already bouncing into the interior of the armored truck.

I limped to my feet in a crouch with my MK II drawn and exited the vehicle. Whoever these guys were, they were well trained. They opened fire on me as soon as I exited.

I tracked their fire, sending two into the chest of one of them and a round to the head of another. More pain tore at my chest and right arm as their rounds found me.

Something hit me in the back of the head so hard, I

spun and saw stars. That was when I saw him above me. Attila tore off his order mask and sneered.

"You thought it was over? You thought you won?" Atilla lifted a heavy boot over my head. "I'm going to crush your skull like an egg."

# THREE

NO WAY I was going out like that. I'd faced aliens, giant bug creatures, and even Atilla himself and beaten him before. My MK II was gone, lost when I was blindsided. My axe and knife still sat snug at my belt. I reached down for the knife hilt but was too slow. As Atilla brought down his boot on my face, a grey blur flashed past my vision.

Butch hit Atilla so hard, I swore she broke him in half. The sounds coming from the female alpha's throat were something truly horrific. The deep growling continued as she ripped into Attila's face and chest.

Echo hunched over Sam's unconscious body, sending shots from his modified shotgun toward the enemy.

Cassie made her way over from the side of the overturned armored car to crouch beside me.

"Did you know about this?" I asked, gripping the handles of my axe and knife so tight, I felt my hands shaking. "Did you know?"

"No," Cassie said, staring me straight in the eye. "I'm sure Julian didn't either. This isn't the Order. This is all Atilla."

I had a decision to make then and there. Either Cassie was a world class liar and she was trying to save her own hide during a failed ambush or she was telling the truth and Atilla was working on his own.

"But if you don't call off Butch, she's going to kill him, and we'll never get our answers," Cassie continued.

I knew she was right; the fight was already over. Echo sent one last round into a dark-clad enemy who tried to head toward the screaming Atilla to help pull Butch off.

"Butch!" I yelled over the sounds of the snarling animal and Attila's screams. "Butch, that's enough."

The animal didn't listen. Butch was lost in some kind of manic frenzy. I could understand that and didn't blame her in the least.

I went over to her, taking her gently by the fur on the nape of her neck.

"Hey, hey, it's me. Look at me, Butch, look at me," I said firmly.

Butch finally let go of Atilla's left arm. Blood soaked

her maw as she panted heavily and whined. Her pupils were tiny dots.

"You did good," I said, wrapping both arms around her neck and slowly walking her back. "You did good. Good girl, thank you."

Butch whined, her eyes never leaving Atilla. I knew if I let her go, she'd finish what she'd started.

Atilla was a bloody mess. His left arm bled through torn black clothes, his chest the same. I could see dull steel through his black shirt. As a Cyber Hunter, the specialized military unit of the Order, Atilla had augmentation across his body. It seemed some kind of metal chestplate had saved his life from Butch.

True to her word, once Butch was free, Cassie stalked over to Atilla. She placed her left boot into his injured arm and applied pressure.

Atilla groaned. He gritted his teeth against the pain.

"Why?" Cassie asked simply.

"He doesn't deserve to lead," Atilla grunted. "Immortal Corp has been our enemy for centuries. Nothing is going to change that. The Order has lost its way."

"Who's working with you?" Cassie asked.

Over their conversation, we could hear the sounds of fight between the GG and the private militia of the rich growing closer. It sounded like the GG was winning and pushing the other forces back toward our location.

"Who!?" Cassie shouted, this time leaning in to press her foot into Atilla's open wounds.

Atilla roared in pain.

"A handful of—a handful of Order members who feel the same way I do." Atilla panted in pain. "Invasion or no invasion, this isn't what we were founded to do. We were meant to rule."

I felt like Butch had finally calmed down enough that she wouldn't try to turn Atilla into wolf chow if I let her go. I released my hold on her neck.

Butch quivered with the promise of more fighting but stood her ground. I looked around the site, recovering my MK II from where it had fallen.

I had an ever-so-slight headache, but I'd live. My body had already healed the worst of my wounds. Sam was just coming around from her concussion. Echo had her propped up against the side of the armored truck.

The sounds of guerilla warfare going on down the street became louder.

"We should move," I told Cassie.

Turning to the side, I spoke into my ear. "X, how much farther to the destination Madam Eternal had in mind?"

"Only a few blocks headed away from the fighting," X answered. "You can make it in twenty minutes if you hurry."

"We go on foot; look for transportation on the way,"

I said, looking down at Atilla. "I don't think we have room for extra travelers."

I pointed my MK II at the side of his head that didn't have the robotic red eye. Odds were that side was still actual skull and brain.

"He has to stand before the Order," Cassie said, removing her boot from his wounded arm. "I know you're not going to like that. I don't either, but it's the way we do things."

She stood directly in my path. I knew her well enough by now to know that she wasn't going to back down. I wasn't about to put a round in her.

"So, what?" I lowered my weapon and shook my head. "We take him with us?"

"He's one of mine," Cassie answered. "He'll be my responsibility. We finish our mission, then we take him back to Dragon Hold until the Voy invasion is over. He should stand trial in front of Julian and the rest of the Order. If there's more involved in this, we'll need him to tell us that as well."

I hated the idea of bringing Atilla anywhere. I didn't even like looking at the guy. Not to mention our fight when the leader of the Corporation coalition was chosen. He walked with an air of disdain about him as if everything was beneath him.

On the other hand, I understood Cassie's need to take him back and interrogate him. If there were members in the Order loyal to Atilla, both she and Julian would want to know who they were.

"All right," I relented. "He's your responsibility."

The sounds of weapon's fire came closer down the streets around us.

"Daniel?" Echo asked.

"I know, time to go," I said.

X laid out the path in front of us, overlaying an augmented reality line for me to follow. I took the lead with Sam and Butch. Cassie wrapped Atilla's wounds and pressed him along in the middle. Echo took up the rear.

"You with us?" I asked, glancing to my left at Sam as we jogged our way down the deserted street. "You took a pretty brutal knock to the head."

"I'll live," Sam answered, removing her helmet from the magnetic belt on her hips. The helmet reminded me more of some ancient knight than anything worn today. She placed it on her head. "I should have put this on while we were in the armored truck."

I nodded.

We made our way in silence, passing only a few civilians this side of the GG line. Most people were trying to get out of the city or holed up in their homes. A few had painted signs about the end of the world and the aliens were our friend. They stood on street corners, wailing as if they were drunk or high on stim, maybe both.

We passed one corner where an older man with no shirt held up a sign that read, "The aliens are our neighbors. Peace." On the board, he had a stick image of the Voy with their four arms.

"Brothers and sisters, the visitors from beyond are not to be considered our enemies," he shouted to us from the opposite end of the street. "Embrace them for who they are. They are our gods."

We had a deadline to meet and we were already behind schedule. Still, I couldn't help but shake my head at the mislead man and mutter under my breath.

"I'm pretty sure God doesn't look like that," I said, thinking of the Voy, the way they tortured prisoners and manipulated the truth, let alone how they grew their soldiers and giant war bugs.

We made it to the next few blocks, traveling at a steady pace until we were in a section of the city where the high rise buildings began to give way to smaller businesses and store fronts.

"This is the place," X said out loud for all to hear. "Two stores up on your right. This is the address Madam Eternal gave us."

I followed X's directions to a two-story building that looked as unassuming as the rest. Clean white stonewalls with windows. No sign on the door.

Echo and Sam secured the street. Cassie stood by with a bound Atilla. I rapped on the door.

Nothing.

Again, this time harder. Butch whined beside me, giving Atilla a death stare then growled. He shied away from her.

"Good giant prehistoric resurrected wolf dog," I told her.

"*Canis lupus alces*," X corrected.

"I'm just going to be honest with you here, X," I responded as I waited in front of the closed door. "I'm never going to remember that. Butch or Lady Butch is as far as I'm going to get."

At that moment, Butch's ears perked up. She cocked her head to the side as if she heard movement from the other side of the door.

I hadn't noticed anything, but I was going to defer to Butch on this one.

"Hello?" I asked. "We were sent by Madam Eternal to collect something."

The door slowly opened.

"You seek the Relic?" an elderly man's voice rasped. I still couldn't see anyone inside. "Are you prepared to assume the mantle and responsibility for an item of such power?"

"Wow, I don't know about all that," I answered. "I'm here to pick up something for Madam Eternal and that's it. And not to be rude, but we're kind of on a schedule. You know, alien invasion coming tomorrow and all."

"Enter," the man said, opening the door wider.

I got my first good look at him. He was tall and pale like he hadn't stepped outside in this decade. Dark hair and sharp features gave him the look of some kind of villain. I knew that was stereotyping, but that was right where my mind went. He wore an expensive-looking older suit with a high collar.

"My name is Mordred and I know of the Relic of which you speak," Mordred said, ushering us in. His eyes lingered on Atilla and the blood dripping from his wounds. "Do you require medical attention?"

"Naw, he's fine," I said, slapping Atilla hard on the back. "He's tougher than he looks. Isn't that right, Cupcake?"

Cassie gave me a hard stare.

"Okay, if you have something to stop his bleeding, it would be helpful, but we really need to go," I said, taking in the room we stepped into. It was old. A musty smell that came from the windows and doors being shut for too long filled the air.

The furniture looked like it belonged in a museum. A coating of dust settled on everything.

Butch sneezed.

"Please take a seat," Mordred said in his slow way of speaking. "I will secure both the Relic and medical supplies. It will only take a moment."

With that, Mordred disappeared into the rear of the building.

"Man, this place gives me the creeps," Sam said quietly. "Are you sure we can trust this guy?"

"Trust is a strong word, but I think that if there's a chance that whatever this Relic is can help us against the Voy, we need to take it," I answered, going over to the window alongside Echo.

The man was the largest member of the Pack protocol, only second to Jax. The whole mission, so far as I could tell, he was trying to do whatever he could to make up to me for his sins in the past. He had been the one to offer to cover Sam when she was unconscious, he took the rear guard as we made our way down the street, and now he took it upon himself to peek out of the musty drapes and act as lookout.

"See anything?" I asked.

"No, but everything here feels wrong." Echo turned to me, shaking his head. "I can't put my finger on it, but it's like—"

A deep growl from Butch cut Echo off. Something under our feet slammed into the floor, sending a tremor through the room.

# FOUR

"WHAT THE HECK IS THAT?" Sam yelled, pulling her bow from her side. The upper and lower portions of her weapon extended. She held an arrow poised ready to fly a moment later.

Echo, Cassie, and I all pointed our weapons to the carpeted floor beneath us.

"Apologize, apologize," Mordred said, entering the room with a book under one arm and a series of vials and bandages in the other. "Nothing to be concerned about. My pet gets restless sometimes while he sleeps. Probably just stretching is all."

*Man, rich people and their money.* I thought back to Rose Cripps being able to resurrect Butch and the wolves. *What kind of animal does Mordred work with?*

I quickly decided I didn't even want to know.

"Is that the Relic?" I asked, holstering my MK II and reaching for the book. "Thanks, we got to get going."

"It is." Mordred handed it over hesitantly. "It's priceless beyond value. The only one of its kind. Whatever you do, do not open it. Take it directly to Madam Eternal. She'll know what to do with it."

I accepted the book, turning it over in my hands. It was a thick volume of pages turned yellow with age. The front and back were a dull crimson red with intricate gold designs. A golden clasp with a simple lock held it shut. There was no title or wording either on the front, back, or spine of the book.

I handed it over to Sam. We fumbled it on the handoff and it fell to the ground with a thud.

Mordred gave us a dirty look.

"Priceless," Mordred repeated as he went over to Atilla to administer the elixir and gauze.

"My bad," I said, leaning over and picking it up for Sam. "Okay, we're on the move as soon as you're done."

Atilla sat still with Cassie on his left and Mordred on his right. His face was pale from the lack of blood.

"Don't touch me with your dark science, wizard." Atilla looked at Mordred with disgust. "I know what you are."

"I very highly doubt that," Mordred said, ignoring Atilla's request. He dipped gauze into a glass bottle filled with bright blue liquid and applied it to Atilla's wounds. "If you did, you'd be much more afraid."

I exchanged looks with Cassie and mouthed the words, "We need to go."

I pointed to the door just to be sure she understood what I was saying.

She nodded.

Lucky for us, Mordred was quick. He placed the medication on Atilla and rewrapped his arm and chest.

In minutes, we were headed out the door again.

"This may be too much to ask, but do you have any kind of transportation we could borrow?" Sam asked Mordred.

"Unfortunately, I do not." Mordred actually looked sad. "I don't get out much. I've been told I need more friends."

"Well, thank you," I said, opening the front door for the rest of the group to exit. "I'll get the book to Madam Eternal, and hopefully, it will help in the coming war with the Voy."

"A decision must be made and it is his to make," Mordred said cryptically, holding my eye as I was about to leave. "You must tell him the truth for his soul to be at rest. If not for you, then for him."

"Riiiiight," I said, not understanding what the old man was saying at all but equally not wanting to stay and engage in further conversation. "Thank you."

I closed the door behind me and we headed out into the midday sun again.

"You idiots. You know what that was?" Atilla asked with a sneer.

"Cassie, can you keep your prisoner under control?" Echo asked. "Or maybe I'll break his jaw and save us all from having to hear his nonsense."

"Mordred is steeped in a dark past of mystery and death," Atilla continued, not caring that Echo just threatened him. "There's a reason no one goes near him. If Madam Eternal is tied up with him somehow, I guarantee you it's not good for anyone."

Outwardly, I ignored Atilla as Cassie told him to shut up. Inwardly, I couldn't help but think there was some truth in what he said. Everything about Mordred felt wrong despite the fact he helped us. Something I couldn't explain touched the back of my neck and sent goosebumps down my spine.

Lucky for us, as we made our way to the Order warehouse, we found a van along the side of the road. Despite the ability to fly being locked down by the GG, we were still able to commandeer the vehicle.

Sam drove this time, with Echo in the front passenger seat. I sat in the back with Butch, who took up so much of the space, it felt cramped. Cassie sat with Atilla in the middle seat.

The streets were now practically empty as we maneuvered through the warehouse district of the city.

Cassie guided us to an unassuming line of steel warehouse structures that looked identical to one another.

"This one," Cassie instructed Sam. "The third one on the right."

Sam pulled up to the warehouse on the deserted street. It was just past midday and my stomach was reminding me of that at the moment. Butch gave me an inquisitive look as my stomach rumbled beside her.

"Handing our enemies the keys to our undoing," Atilla said as we piled out. "Have you and Julian gone completely insane?"

"You're everything that's wrong with the Order and their old ways of thought," Cassie told her counterpart. "You see enemies where there are only allies. You think we need to fight amongst ourselves, when the real enemy attacks tomorrow."

We moved to the wide double doors of the steel structure. Cassie placed a palm on a digital reader, as well as entered a combination with so many digits, I was surprised she could remember them all. Next, a blue light scanned her body from top to bottom.

"The Order doesn't mess around," X said in my ear. "I'm scanning the building now and I'm finding so many automated defenses, it's on par with Dragon Hold. This place is a small fortress. If Cassie were anything but who she said she was, we'd be a smear on the ground."

"Comforting thoughts," I murmured as the door opened from the middle and slid back ever so slowly. The steel doors widened just enough to allow us entrance.

"This is true insanity." Atilla refused to go in when Cassie pushed him forward. "This—about what you're doing. To give them the keys to the world engine is—"

A sound like a pair of blades being drawn from their sheaths cut Atilla off. As a Cyber Hunter herself, Cassie had her own augmentations on her body. Her right forearm was completely robotic. From it, a pair of blades sprouted. She pressed them against Atilla's back.

"Move or I'll skewer you where your own metal won't shield," Cassie told him. "I want you alive, but I don't *need* you alive."

The menace in her voice caused me to raise my eyebrows and exchange looks with Sam and Echo. It was easy to forget at times that the dark-haired beauty was as deadly as any member of the Pack Protocol.

Atilla rethought his position then obeyed. One by one, we entered the warehouse doors. What we found inside took my breath away.

If I thought the armory in Dragon Hold was something to be seen, I didn't know how to describe what I was seeing now. It was like an amusement park for weapons enthusiasts.

Racks and rows of firearms, explosives, bladed

weapons, and body armor opened in front of us from where we stood to the opposite side of the building.

"Holy smokes," Echo said under his breath. "There has to be enough hardware in here to equip an army."

"This is most impressive, but how are we going to take all of this with us?" Sam asked. "We aren't exactly flying a dropship. Even then, there's enough in here for a fleet of dropships to carry."

"This isn't what we're here for." Cassie waved us to follow. "This gear will be useful in the fight, but Julian will see that it's moved to the battlefield if we need it. The World Engine is in the back."

*Relics, World Engines; we're really pulling out all the stops,* I thought to myself. *But maybe this is what it's going to take to defeat the Voy. All of us working together with everything we've got.*

"Years in development and billions of credits later, and we hand our most powerful weapon over to the enemy," Atilla said through gritted teeth. "Our ancestors would be turning over in their graves if they could see you now."

"Your ancestors," Cassie answered. "Not all of us had the pristine upbringing you did."

"You're a dog," Atilla spat at Cassie. "Julian should have never brought you into the Order. You're not one of us."

I kind of wanted to punch him for that, but Cassie ignored him, shoving him forward to walk faster. After

Mordred had stopped his bleeding, Cassie had secured his hands behind his back with a slender piece of metal she produced from the folds of her black cloak.

We traveled down the rows of weapons to a cylinder-shaped podium where a metal briefcase floated in some kind of stasis.

Cassie walked to the podium, entering yet another code. A pad folded out from the podium with a small needle. Without hesitation, she pricked her finger.

"I hate needles," Sam said beside me.

The security measure accepted Cassie's blood. A moment later, the suitcase floated to the podium desk in front of her.

"Great, we're going to kill an alien army with an old book and a suitcase," Echo grumbled. "What do we go pick up next? The card deck of destiny?"

"What is the World Engine?" I asked Cassie. "What's in the briefcase?"

"The World Engine is a satellite orbiting Mars," Cassie informed us, opening the suitcase with awe. "The briefcase holds the controls to the satellite. The World Engine holds a giant tungsten rod that, when shot from space, will impact Mars with more force than any known explosion."

We all stood stunned.

"We'll be able to cripple the Voy forces before we even engage, maybe even destroy them altogether," Cassie answered. "It should be used as a first line of defense. It's never been tested, but if the Voy get too close to the city, we won't be able to use it at all in fear that we'll cause damage to our own forces."

My mind did backflips thinking about the repercussions of such a weapon.

"What were you going to do with it if the Voy hadn't attacked?" Sam asked. "What was the Order willing to do?"

"That's the billion-credit question, Red." Atilla smirked. "Tell them, Cassie. Tell your new friends what the Order was really planning."

"Shut up," Cassie warned.

"What? Now that the Immortal Corp idiots have actually asked a worthwhile question, we aren't their best friends anymore?" Atilla prodded. "Tell them, Cassie. Tell them it was a doomsday device in case things got out of hand. Tell them what we are willing to do."

# FIVE

CASSIE HIT Atilla so hard in the stomach, I thought his guts must have had to touch the back of his spine.

"Shut up," Cassie growled as Atilla fell to his knees gasping.

Echo and Sam looked toward me. We were all wondering the same thing. Was Atilla telling the truth? Did the Order construct the World Engine to act as an end of times weapon?

Cassie didn't miss the looks.

"I'm not hiding anything," Cassie said, opening the briefcase in her hands for us to see. Inside was a flat control panel with a holographic feed, a series of buttons, and a security device I had never seen before. "This is the most powerful weapon we know of. We created it to act as insurance if things got really bad."

"Really bad with whom?" Echo asked what we were all thinking.

"The GG, another corporation, Immortal Corp," Cassie finished honestly. "Let's not forget we're not exactly the good guys in this story. We all have our own agendas. Judge me if you will, but I didn't want to lie."

We stood there in silence for a long moment. No one wanted to agree with her, but she was right. We weren't heroes or the good guys in this story. We were what was left, just broken people with broken pasts trying to do the right thing here and now.

"I know the dropships are all tied up taking gear and people to the forward station outside the city, but I think this case calls for a ride," Sam said, leaving to make the call. "I don't want to have to drive back through the city."

"No argument here," Echo said, roughly yanking Atilla from his kneeling position to an upright one. "I'll secure our friend."

Cassie closed the briefcase in her hands with a sigh.

"Is it always going to be like this?" Cassie asked, placing the briefcase at her feet and taking a seat on the ground. "Fighting each other, fighting invaders, fighting the GG?"

I didn't know what to say, if Cassie even wanted an answer or if it was a rhetorical question. Butch nudged me hard in the ribs.

I looked down at her and I swore she lifted an eyebrow at me then tilted her jaw toward Cassie.

"I don't know if violence is ever going to not cast a shadow on our lives, maybe just who we choose as our opponents," I answered Cassie honestly. I ran a hand over my jaw. The stubble there prickled my fingers as I took a seat next to her. "What did Atilla mean when he said you weren't really one of them?"

"We may die tomorrow, so screw secrets, right?" Cassie leaned back, her arms planted on the ground behind her. "The Order has a few members whose heritage can be traced back to those who started the group. Atilla's family is one of the oldest."

"Why'd you join?" I asked. "You don't seem like Atilla."

Cassie laughed out loud.

"I'll take that as a compliment." Cassie chewed on her lower lip, studying me intently. I could tell there was an internal debate waging behind those dark eyes of hers. She was deciding how much to tell me.

"Give her some space," X coached in my head. "Not really, but if you give her the option, I think she'll talk."

I couldn't respond to X without letting Cassie know she was giving me advice.

"I know this is getting personal," I said, preparing to stand and go check on Sam and the status of the dropship. "If you'd rather not talk about it, I'm good with that."

Cassie reached out with her right hand and grabbed my left before I could get up. Her palm was calloused and rough. Exactly what I would have expected from a warrior who lived a tough life.

What I didn't expect was the strength with which she pulled me back. It wasn't forceful but firm.

"No, please, stay," Cassie said, swallowing hard. She looked at our hands as if realizing for the first time we were making contact. She quickly released her grip. "Sorry—sorry, I'm not—I've been told in the past I push people away. I don't want to, but it's hard for me to talk about my past."

"I understand," I answered, keeping my seat. "You can lie to me about your past if you want. If it makes you feel better, I'll just believe whatever you tell me."

Cassie cracked another grin. She looked around to make sure we were out of hearing distance from the others.

Sam was near the front entrance on the comm line. Echo secured Atilla to a shelf stacked with armor down the aisle from us.

"I grew up on the moon with a father who left before I was born and a mother who drank too much." Cassie shook her head. "I think she tried in her own way. There were good times in there between when she woke up in the morning and when she got drunk again. I started working early to support us. Waitressing seemed like a natural fit for a girl with no education.

One day, a few customers were getting too friendly with me. Julian stepped in and made sure they never bothered me again."

Cassie paused in her story now. The way she looked off in the distance, the tone in her voice told me she wasn't just telling me the story; she was reliving events in her past.

"I didn't know for a long time why Julian helped me," Cassie continued slowly. "Years later, I found out he had a daughter that would have been my age, but that's his story to tell. Anyway, he took me in. He trained me to not only be a member of the Order, but one of their elite, a Cyber Hunter."

"The process seems painful," I said, looking at the section of her forearm poking out of her black coat that was metal instead of skin. "Was it worth it?"

"You know, I've asked myself that before," Cassie said, looking down at her forearms. "Yes, even despite the madness of an alien invasion, it's all been worth it. The Order has shown me who I really am. I would never have known how strong I can be if I wasn't pushed. Mankind's greatest enemy isn't aliens or one another; it's themselves and falling into a comfortable life of mediocrity."

"Wow, that's really deep," I said, trying and succeeding in getting Cassie to smile again.

"I try," she answered. "How about you?"

"My memory is still coming back, but I know

enough now to say I was an orphan, recruited into the Pack Protocol Program basically because I'm stubborn. They call it a fighting spirit, but let's just be honest," I said, thinking back on what I did know of my past and the many areas that were still blank. "I know a Way follower named Enoch who believes everything happens for a reason whether we can see that now or not. Maybe we both had to go through what we did to be the forces we are today to turn back the Voy."

"You really think we can defeat them?"

"I know we can. We have to."

The lull in conversation grew into complete silence as we were each lost to our own thoughts. I'd been part of silences that were uncomfortable before. This one wasn't. We each sat thinking about our words and reveling in the feeling of sharing ourselves with someone else. It wasn't exactly like we went to group therapy for this kind of stuff.

As much as I hated to admit it, it felt good to have this kind of meaningful conversation.

"What are you going to do after this?" Cassie finally broke the spell of silence. "I mean, you can't exactly go back to Immortal Corp, unless you decide to try and be the one to take over the corporation."

"Have you met me?" I asked with an arched brow. "I don't even lead the meeting with the corporations now. I have no desire to sit behind a desk for the rest of my life. Not really my style."

"And maybe that's exactly why you need to be the one to lead," Cassie said.

I had the feeling she would have gone on, but Sam approached, the helmet still on her head.

"Dropship is en route," Sam explained loud enough for Echo and Atilla to hear from their positions. "We'll be taken directly to the staging area outside the city. Let's hope these two weapons we picked up are going to be enough to turn the tide of battle. Reports are coming that the Voy are massing."

Cassie and I rose to our feet.

"You should let me go now," Atilla said with a smug shrug. Which was hard to do since his hands were tied behind his back, but he still managed to pull it off. "My family will be looking for me soon enough. They'll contact Julian and then you'll have to fight a battle on two fronts."

"Julian leads the Order," Cassie said, going up to him. I thought she might punch him again. Apparently, so did he. He shied away from her. "You manipulated a handful of Order soldiers to their death. That was it. You have your mommy and daddy who'll try and come get you, but Julian leads."

Atilla looked like he was going to say something else.

Cassie unsheathed the twin blades from the top of her right forearm.

Thinking better of his next action, Atilla closed his mouth.

Together, we walked to the front doors of the warehouse. Minutes later, a dropship landed in the street in front of the warehouse.

Julian himself was there. The tall man wore all black with a long black coat. I realized that if he was a Cyber Hunter himself, I had yet to see his upgrades. Stone-eyed, he glared at Atilla.

For his part, Atilla walked with his head down. Echo shoved him into the back of the open dropship. Sam carried the tome we recovered for Madam Eternal inside.

Butch followed while Cassie stopped, World Engine in hand, to speak with Julian.

I didn't mean to eavesdrop, except that I did.

I paused before entering the dropship. The craft's thrusters hummed just low enough for me to be able to hear.

"They know why the weapon was built," Cassie told Julian. "And that's not even our biggest problem. Madam Eternal is working with Mordred. Whatever happens, we can't let her open that book."

# SIX

THE FLIGHT to the staging area outside the city was short and smooth. It was probably the first thing that had gone to plan in a long time.

The base camp was set up in the path of the Voy if they were to take a direct route from their base to the city. We were monitoring their activity now. If they tried to send a force around us, we'd know. But I had an itch in the back of my mind that told me the Voy were not afraid of a full-out fight in the slightest.

I had seen the soldiers they grew. I saw their aircrafts and the giant bugs they would use as weapons. The Voy were sure of their victory.

Since the bulk of the Galactic Government fleet was still en route, things were shaping up to be one heck of a fight. The pendulum kept swinging in and out of our favor as new weapons were produced by our allies.

The World Engine from the Order was sure to put a hurt on the Voy. The mech suits from Phoenix gave us a chance against the Voy bugs.

What I was most interested in was the book we picked up for Madam Eternal. Sam carried it under her arm easy enough. Cassie's comment to Julian made me second guess myself on whether it was a smart move to hand it over to Madam Eternal no questions asked.

The way Cassie snuck glances at it now told me I wouldn't have to wait long to find out what was inside.

We ate a meal of pre-loaded protein packs that tasted like mush, but it did the job.

We touched down at the forward base as the sun began to lower behind the endless dunes of the Martian planet. The dropship settled onto the sandy ground with a slight tremor. The rear hatches opened to let us off.

What I saw when I exited the back of the dropship was amazing. I had seen a forward base erected in hours before when we came to the GG's aid at the Way Settlement.

That was impressive. This was a miracle. Thousands of tents had popped up in the space of a single day. Corporations that were previously enemies were working side by side to stack equipment, erect even more tents, and check gear.

"Amazing what can be done when we share a common mind," a voice said to my left.

I looked over to see Enoch with his clean-shaven head and white robes beaming at me.

"Sure this is the best place for you to be?" I asked. "Things are going to get dicey real soon."

"The fight isn't going to take place here," Enoch said, opening his arms to the swirling mass of people running to and from various jobs. "But this is where I'll be needed the most. This encampment will act as a medical bay when the fighting begins."

I now understood what he was doing here. Enoch wasn't exactly a warrior, but that didn't mean he was a coward either. He was going to find a place to share his skill set.

Echo, Sam, Cassie, and Atilla piled out of the back of the dropship with me. We all made our way from the landing strip, where a myriad of dropships were docked ready for deployment.

There had to be hundreds of them all lined up like soldiers themselves.

As we walked farther into the tent city, I got an idea of how large this operation really was. Tents, both square and circular of various colors and sporting different sigils, popped up in tight configuration. Most of the tents were black or dark red to blend in with the sand.

The Phoenix tents to my right were white. A Galactic Government tent wore the golden menacing feline sigil.

Enoch wasn't wrong; it was a sight to see. So many factions each with their own agenda working as one. Maybe we needed an alien invasion sooner if this was the outcome.

"Did you recover the book?" Madam Eternal asked, emerging from a narrow alley of two tents.

It seemed the chill in the air didn't bother her in the least. She stood straight backed, poised and regal as ever, her blood-red cloak trailing behind her.

"We did," I said, motioning to Sam to stop as she moved to hand over the tome . "Do you mind if I ask you what's in it?"

Julian had joined our group with a pair of Order soldiers. He handed off Atilla to them and stood with Cassie ready to intervene.

"Our salvation," Madam Eternal said simply enough. She took a step forward, her hands reaching for the book under Sam's arm.

"Do not give her that book." Julian stepped up, placing himself between Sam and Madam Eternal. "You do not know its power."

Sam, who had removed her helmet in the dropship, looked at me with an arched brow.

"X, what can you tell me about the book?" I asked low enough for only her to hear.

Madam Eternal and Julian locked eyes.

"I don't have any records of the exact volume," X

answered in my head. She hurried through her explanation, understanding that the situation was reaching its boiling point. "It's old, from Earth when it was still inhabitable, no doubt. Thirteenth, maybe Fourteenth century."

"I'm not used to explaining myself," Madam Eternal said with a smile that wasn't friendly in the least. "I requested the book. Daniel was kind enough to retrieve it. The book will be used against the Voy as a last resort. It may be our only means of victory."

"You don't think I know what that book is?" Julian growled. "I've heard stories of the Relics. Whispers and rumors that they even existed, but if you want it, I know everything I heard was true."

"So you are allowed your weapons and I am not to have mine?" Madam Eternal eyed the briefcase in Cassie's arms. "Seems a little one-sided, Julian. We both want the same thing here. We want to survive. This has all been about survival. It always will be."

The stand-off was gathering a crowd now as more and more bystanders stopped their work or slowed their walk as they made their way to see the head of the Order and Madam Eternal going at it.

"The World Engine will be enough to stop them," Julian finally answered. "It'll wreak havoc on their numbers. Whatever is left of them that gets through, we'll deal with. There is no need to open a Relic."

I couldn't hold my tongue anymore. Listening to the

two argue was like being a third party to a debate on the latest holo flick that I didn't watch.

"Throw up a hand if you're confused," I said, lifting my own hand. Echo and Sam followed. Butch yipped. "Would you two like to share with the rest of the class what you're going on about?"

"The book in question is a Relic. It has been said that these Relics have power not of this world and they always come with a price," Julian answered without taking his eyes off Madam Eternal. It was almost as if he expected her to make a move at any time to grab the tome. "The Order has been alive for centuries. Ancient texts of our organization speak of items like this Relic lost to time. It should be buried. Better yet destroyed."

"You fear what you do not understand." Madam Eternal clicked her tongue. With a right hand, she reached into the fold of her robes.

Immediately, Cassie pointed her right forearm, capable of sending out a projectile, at the woman. Julian drew a blaster from a holster at the small of his back in the blink of an eye.

Echo moved to take a protective stance in front of Sam, not that she needed it.

"As far as I know, we are all still allies here despite the fact we may disagree," the madam said, removing a long hairpin from the inside folds of her cloak. "If I wanted you dead, you would be dead."

The mysterious woman leaned down to draw a large circle in the sand in front of her.

"Of all that there is to know, in the billions of galaxies in our ever expanding universe, how much do you think you all know and comprehend today?" Madam Eternal looked at each of us in turn. The fact there were weapons pointed at her face did nothing to discourage or intimidate her. "Go ahead, how much do you think everyone who is here knows of all that there is to know? One percent, ten, twenty-five?"

"Minimal," I answered. "A very small fraction at most."

"Exactly." Madam Eternal made a very small circle inside the much larger one. "The large circle represents all there is to know or that can be known. The smaller one is what we do know."

She then went on to motion to the space outside the smaller circle but still within the larger one.

"This empty space is where things like Relics, and more exactly, this book lie," Madam Eternal explained. "Just because you do not understand what it is or what it does, does not make it wrong."

"Explain it to us, then," Cassie asked, lowering her arm. "Tell us what it is."

Julian lowered his weapon.

"It is a gateway to another time in space," Madam Eternal answered. "A time and place where there are allies that would help us win this fight."

"And you understand how this gateway works, who or what will come from the other side, how to close it, the repercussions of opening a rift in space?" Julian asked incredulously. "No, you do not. I can see that in your eyes."

For the first time, something like rolling anger flashed across Madam Eternal's expression. I knew then that Julian was right. Madam Eternal, for all her knowledge, did not have exact answers for us.

I was caught in the middle of an alien invasion and opening a rift in reality. One thing I did know was that I had to put an end to the squabbling now. We had earned ourselves a crowd. Right now, we needed to focus on the tasks to prepare for the enemy, not in-fighting amongst our own leaders.

"I'll secure the book," I told both of them, making eye contact with both Julian and Madam Eternal. "This entire conversation could be for nothing. We use the World Engine and we fight. Let's pray it doesn't come down to this Relic, but if it does, I'm with Madam Eternal on this one. We use it only as a last resort if we have to."

I didn't think that was the answer either party wanted, but it seemed to be at least agreeable to each one of them.

Julian nodded toward me.

"We've picked the right person to lead, it seems."

Madam Eternal gave me a slight head bow. "If and when the time comes I'll be ready to use the book."

"If and when," I repeated.

The crowd began to disperse and Madam Eternal moved closer to me. Her voice was low but still above a whisper as if she didn't mind others hearing, but her words were initially intended for me.

"There is power in knowing one's true name," Madam Eternal said quickly. "I know yours, Daniel Hunt, and you should know mine. Carly Cefrin is the name I was given when born. I am known by that name in certain parts of the Earth and Moon should we be victorious here and you need to find me again."

"Wish we could have met under better circumstances, Carly," I said with a nod of appreciation.

She gave me a knowing smile with a twinkle in her eye and left my side.

I moved through the crowd with Sam, Echo, and Butch beside me.

Cassie caught my eye and gave me an approving wink before heading over to Julian. No doubt they had a lot to discuss, not only about the Relic, but about Atilla as well.

"Daniel, hey, Daniel," a young woman's voice called out.

My stomach sank. It was Cryx.

The young woman I still thought of as a girl waved

me over from down a row of tents to my right. She stood in the open flaps of a large circular tent that had two crests of the Pack Protocol wolf falling down the sides.

"What in god's name of—"

I saw a Way settler look at me with open mouth waiting to hear how I was going to finish the curse.

"—dangerously high caf are you doing here?"

"Good to see you too." Cryx's eyes went huge when she caught sight of Butch. "Wow, it's true. You got a horse and a wolf to mate."

"She's just a wolf, *canis lupimus* somthingmus," I answered. "What are you doing here?"

"Someone needed to take care of you and your stuff," Cryx said in a motherly tone. "Bapz can't leave Dragon Hold, so it's up to me. Please, enter."

I walked into the tent with the rest of the crew. I was still adamant about sending Cryx back, but I had to be honest: she did a great job setting up the place. The tent was larger on the inside than I would have guessed. Fabric walls sectioned it off, creating a sitting place in the middle and various rooms that circled the middle area.

It even had a homey kind of feel to it with our sigil all over the place and lounging furniture in the middle with enough food to make my stomach rumble in greed.

"I know how much you like food and caf." Cryx beamed.

"Listen, this is going to be a war zone. You can't—" I cut myself off as my eyes gravitated to a large steel container on ice. It sat on top of a table in the center of the room. "Is that what I think it is?"

Echo walked over, putting a cup on the table beneath it and pulled the lever handle that was in the shape of a wolf head. Ice cold caf poured out the nozzle.

"High Octane Iced Caf." Cryx shrugged. "But I mean, if you want me to go, I guess I should pack everything up and take it with me back to Dragon Hold."

"I vote she stays," Echo said over his shoulder as he moved on from the caf to the table of food.

"Me too." Sam grabbed a sandwich and plopped herself wearily in one of the chairs. She used the Relic as a table for her meal. "Don't you think you're being a little overprotective, Daniel?"

"Hey, she's my responsibility and just a kid," I asserted, going over to the cold caf machine myself. "It's not safe here."

"I'm not a kid," Cryx complained. "Besides, what safer place could there be? I mean, I'm surrounded by half the Corporations and the GG."

Screams from somewhere in our own tent ended the conversation.

# SEVEN

I TURNED my neck so fast, I thought I was going to give myself whiplash. The screams and moans were interspersed with words now.

"No! Stop—I can—I can save you," the choked male voice continued.

"Who's in here with us?" I demanded, moving toward one of the draped sections of our tent.

"Preacher, it's Preacher. He was just lying down," Cryx answered.

I sprinted to the closed off section and drew back the curtain, followed by Echo, Sam, and a barking Butch.

Preacher lay on a cot. Beads of sweat ran down his brow into his beard. The one eye I could see not hidden by his patch squinted painfully as he continued to toss and turn.

No more words escaped his lips, but rather, animalistic grunts and growls.

Butch whined.

"Easy, easy there," Sam said, sitting at the edge of his bed. She gently shook his shoulders. "Preacher, wake up. You have to wake up now."

Preacher quieted, opening his eye. He stared at Sam for a moment, confused.

"Karen, is that you?" Preacher asked, a hint of hope in his words. "Is that really you?"

"No, Preacher, it's me, Samantha," Sam said in a sad voice. "It's just me."

"Oh." Preacher went from looking hopeful to confused then embarrassed as he took the rest of us in. "Bad dream, I guess."

Preacher propped himself up in the bed, licking his dry lips. Perspiration soaked his sheets and shirt despite the cold night coming on.

"I'll get you some water," Echo said, leaving the room.

It was strange for me to see the hardened veteran I had known wielding his bright sword against his foes like the master he was, now screaming in his sleep.

The Voy experimented on Preacher during his time in captivity. Somehow, they had managed to neutralize his healing ability.

After they roughed him up pretty badly, Preacher was still healing from his wounds. He looked better and he could get around now with the help of crutches. The bruises on his face were fading, cuts scabbing over.

"I guess I was just having a nightmare," Preacher said, cleaning the sweat from his face.

"We all have those days," Sam said, removing her gaze from Preacher and looking over at me. "Maybe Daniel's the lucky one after all. He doesn't have to remember all those years with Immortal Corp where we acted as their killing machines."

I didn't know what to say. There was a lot to unwrap in that one comment. When Preacher heard about Amber's supposed death, he was the one who wiped my memory and dropped me on the moon.

I understood he was doing it to protect me. I would have gotten myself killed acting in a rage of vengeance. I had even forgiven him for it, although I hadn't told him that yet.

"Here you go," Echo said, returning with a cup of water. "Get this in you."

"Thanks," Preacher said, consuming the water in a single draught. "Some nights it's worse than others."

"You ever keep track of how many you killed?" Echo asked. "I can still see all their faces."

I looked at Cryx, who stood awkwardly by the open curtain flap to Preacher's section of the tent. I wasn't sure if she should be hearing this, but maybe it would be good for her. She wanted to fight; she should know what came after.

"I try not to think about it," Sam said, swallowing hard. "Try, but I still do."

"I've taken forty-seven lives for certain with my blade," Preacher said with a hollow voice. "I only count those I saw face to face as the life left their body. It doesn't seem right to count them if they had helmets or masks on."

Preacher said this devoid of any joy. He was simply stating a fact. A fact that it sounded like he had thought about more than once.

The room in the tent quieted as we all thought back on the sins of our past.

"There's nothing I can do about the past," I said, breaking the silence. "All we can do is move forward. I don't think balancing the scales is an option at this point, but taking on the Voy is a step in the right direction."

"The things that made us animals are the very reason we're able to stand against other evils as well," Sam chimed in with a nod in my direction. "We saw that when we saved my city in the Badlands."

"It takes a monster to kill a monster," Echo added. "Not sure where I heard that one, but it fits here."

"Sorry to interrupt, but Wesley Cage is requesting a meeting with you and the rest of the heads of the Corporations and the Galactic Government," X said inside my head. "They think the Voy will come at first light. The sun is nearly set now."

"Thanks, X," I answered, taking my leave from those in the room.

Before I left, I knew I had to make peace with Preacher. When the fighting started, there was no knowing who was going to make it out alive. I had enough regrets to live with. I wasn't going to make more.

"Preacher," I said, turning back before I left the room. "I understand why you did it."

Relief spread over the old man's face like a tension I didn't know he was holding was lifted.

He gave me a smile and a nod. "Thank you, Danny."

That was it. That was about as much emotional healing the two of us could stomach. I turned to go, leaving a confused Echo, Sam, and Cryx in my wake. Butch trotted beside me as we made our way from the tent.

X was right. The sun had set. All that separated us from war now was a single night. If the Voy kept their promise, and I had no reason to think otherwise, the Martian sand would be soaked in the blood of humans and aliens very soon.

"You did the right thing," X said, directing me with a map to where the meeting was taking place. "I mean, for Preacher. You should do the same for Echo. He still thinks he killed Amber and he's living with that."

"Crip, X, are you my friend or my conscience?" I

asked good-naturedly. "No one can know that she's alive. I mean, the fact Cassie and the Order know is already too many people. The only way she stays safe is if everyone thinks she's dead."

"I understand, but you see how hard Echo is trying to make amends," X answered, closing the conversation. "Just something to keep in mind."

"I will," I acquiesced.

We made it the rest of the way through the tent city in silence. Well, at least silence on our ends. It seemed a dropship or fighter squadron flew overhead every few minutes.

I watched as a group of dropships towing Phoenix armor mechs with heavy cables passed. The walking tanks of armor where masterpieces of war. If I made it out of this alive, I had to figure out how to get my hands on one of those.

Galactic Government soldiers as well as personnel from every corporation present jogged, walked, or ran to and from their assignments. The air was alive with the electricity only the promise of a battle could bring.

I soon found myself at an unmarked tent, guarded by a pair of Shadow Praetorians. They must have been left with instructions not to give me a hard time, because when they saw me, they opened the tent flaps. Or who knows, maybe it was the giant wolf walking with me that made them rethink holding me up.

I was getting used to the stares and gawks as Butch walked with me.

Moving inside, we found a long table with enough chairs to seat our war council as well as the newest addition to our group and his contingent, Colonel Jonah Strife.

The last time I had seen the colonel, we were defending his retreat as he pulled out of an ambush by the Voy. Now he sat talking with Wesley Cage at the table, a major I didn't recognize on his left and Captain Zoe Valentine on his right.

Zoe had been our contact with the Galactic Government when the identity of the Voy was revealed. She was a hard woman I had fought beside on the moon while she was on prison transport duty to Earth.

Also in the room were Madam Eternal, Commander Shaw from Phoenix, Julian, and Cassie. I couldn't help but notice that Madam Eternal and the members from the Order were on opposite sides of the room.

Tension was high to say the least. It was going to be an interesting war council.

When I arrived, Zoe stood from her seat and made a beeline for me. She extended a hand and pressed it hard when I accepted.

"Thank you," she said. She wore her mustard-colored armor, customary in the GG. "You kept your word and got our men out safe. I just wish I could have been there to help."

"Well, you're here now," I answered. "We'll need you."

Zoe nodded.

"How's that daughter of yours?" I asked.

Zoe reached inside her armor chestplate to reveal a golden chain. On the end of the chain was what looked like a locket in the shape of a tiny book. She opened it. I saw the freckled face of a young girl. The girl looked like a spitting image of her mother.

"She's safe and off planet." Zoe smiled down at the picture. "I was able to get her off Mars before the flood of elites here tried to make their escape. It's chaos out there."

"Oh, I know," I agreed, thinking back to my own saunter in the streets of Athens. "I'm glad your daughter is safe for her sake and for yours. You'll be able to concentrate and focus on what needs to be done here and now, knowing she's in good hands."

"She's on the moon with her grandmother." Zoe sighed. "You're right about being able to focus. If we're going to defeat the aliens, we'll need to work as one."

During our conversation, Colonel Strife had also risen from his seat and came over to pump my hand.

"Sorry for the intrusion, Captain," Colonel Strife said to Zoe. "I just wanted to thank Daniel for seeing us out of that ambush the other night."

I shook the man's hand warmly.

*Do you ask about Project Nemesis?* I wondered to myself

as I held my smile intact. *Why not? You're not used to playing it safe anyway.*

"I'm just glad we were able to get you and your team out," I answered honestly. "But I do wonder what happened to the man you had in custody. The one called Nemesis."

# EIGHT

IT WAS like I poured a bucket of ice water over the colonel. His expression went from one of shock to troubled. After a moment, he looked over his right and then left shoulder.

"Sir, I can go if you need me to." Zoe shot me a look that said, 'What the heck are you doing?' as she addressed her superior.

"No, that won't be necessary," Colonel Strife answered. "Mr. Hunt witnessed what few have and what none may ever again."

"Why's that?" I asked, thinking of the shirtless man who looked like an older version of myself. The Galactic Government had done some kind of experimentation on him, that much was clear enough. Anything past that was speculation.

"The man you saw has yet to be recovered," Colonel Strife stated simply. "Right now, we have larger issues at hand. I'm sure once we defeat the Voy, an initiative to apprehend him will begin, but Project Nemesis was always General Armstrong's interest. He led that arm of research. Since he's no longer with us, I imagine Project Nemesis will be closed."

General Armstrong had been killed during the Voy ambush the previous night. Nemesis had made his escape after I released him from his collar, and to be honest, I didn't blame him. Who knows what he had been subjected to and how willing he had been to undergo the experiments.

"If we could begin," Wesley called from the head of the table. He motioned me forward to take the lead seat. "Daniel, you were chosen to lead this coalition. With the Galactic Government joining us, I think that should remain the same."

All eyes in the room swung over to Colonel Jonah Strife.

"The Galactic Government has no issue with that as long as we agree on any moves before they are made," the colonel responded, taking his seat. "Please, proceed."

I moved to take my position at the front of the table, with Wesley, Commander Shaw, Madam Eternal and the Order on my left, the GG on my right.

How we had gotten here was a true miracle. One I

would have to sit back and write down one day once all the madness decided to take a vacation. That wasn't happening any time soon. Not nearly soon enough.

All eyes looked at me. I wasn't much for speeches and I wasn't going to start now.

"Where are we?" I asked, looking at Wesley. "Voy movements?"

"We've been monitoring them from afar and now in conjunction with the Galactic Government's help," Wesley advised everyone at the table. "They're mobilizing outside of their camouflage barrier. As far as we can tell, they have no plan but to do exactly what they said, hit us tomorrow and hit us hard."

"Do we have a better idea of their strength?" Julian asked.

"Still unknown since only a portion of their forces are moving outside of their shielding and we know they have an underground structure," Wesley answered. "Another unknown is their line of attack. The most direct route would lead them here to Athens. That's why we've set our forward base to intercept them."

"But they could move anywhere and we would need to adjust our defensive position to intercept them," Commander Shaw finished the thought. "Or perhaps they attack multiple locations at once."

"That would divide our forces," I thought out loud. "That would be the smart thing to do."

"The rest of the Galactic Government?" Madam

Eternal posed the question to Colonel Strife. "When can we expect them to arrive?"

"We're spread out over two planets and the moon," Colonel Strife reported. "Ten percent of our forces stationed on Earth, thirty percent on Mars, and sixty percent on the moon, where the majority of the population resides. Still, we'll be more than enough for the Voy. Reinforcements won't get here until tomorrow night. Depending on when the Voy attack, it'll most likely be too late. But have no fear, we can do this. We are enough."

I couldn't help but think Colonel Strife should be the one leading the conversation. He practically exuded confidence. His words made me want to fight the Voy right now.

"We'll need the bulk of the GG to partner with the Order pilots and help us in the air," Wesley confirmed, looking down at a datapad in front of him. "That's where we'll be most vulnerable."

"We can cover you from the sky," the major next to Jonah who hadn't spoken yet chimed in. He was young with jet black hair and armor so clean, I'd eat off it. "We have the best pilots this side of the known galaxy."

"Major Tetch will be leading our initiative from the air," Colonel Strife introduced him. "We'll be ready for them."

I didn't know Tetch from Adam, but I liked the kid.

He was eager and ready to begin. He had an honest face, if that meant anything. I tried not to judge a drop-ship by its paint job, but sometimes that was all you had to go on.

"We should use the World Engine now," Cassie filled the silence. "We can handicap them, maybe even take the fight out of them altogether before the fighting actually starts."

Inquiring eyes looked at both members of the Order.

"The World Engine is a satellite capable of dropping a megaton of spear-like steel from orbit," Julian said with a straight face. "Upon impact, it will decimate an area up to a hundred kilometers in every direction."

"And this is—legal?" Zoe asked from her seat.

I could practically feel the moment grow in tension as the three members representing the Galactic Government straightened in their seats.

"It's necessary," Julian intervened. "And when it saves thousands of lives, everyone will be glad we developed it."

"We should make an effort to stay on point here," Commander Shaw voiced before more questions of the legality of a private corporation developing a weapon like this could be made. "Let's deal with the enemy first then we can discuss other matters once humanity cements its place in the rest of history."

That logic was difficult to argue.

"We could drop it on them now, but we should wait to make sure they attack," Wesley addressed Cassie's first question. "If there is even a one-percent chance something could happen that would cause them to rethink their decision, we need to afford them that chance. Once they mobilize and begin their assault, then I think we owe it to everyone to use the World Engine."

"I feel like we've given them enough chances at this point, but if it makes you feel better, we can issue one last order to stand down when they come," I said from my seat. "If they refuse to back down, then let's unleash the Order's toy."

"How many of these World Engine rounds do you have at your disposal?" Colonel Strife asked.

"Just one," Julian answered

"Let's pray that's enough." Colonel Strife sighed heavily. "Corporations with weapons in orbit, aliens, super soldiers, and secret projects. What's next?"

I didn't think this was the time to bring up Madam Eternal's book, but I couldn't help myself. The ornery side of me won out.

"We may have another ace up our sleeve if things get real bad," I said, ignoring the shocked expressions on Julian's and Cassie's faces. "Madam Eternal has a final option in case all is lost."

Wesley scratched the back of his head. Commander Shaw gave me an amused look as everyone else turned to Madam Eternal for an explanation.

"You just had to," X said in my head. "You love to cause trouble."

"This should be good," I murmured under my breath. "Couldn't help myself."

"Daniel's right." Madam Eternal was the only one who seemed not to be put off by my comment. "There is a book that would connect our world to others. Help will come and we will use it as a last resort just like Daniel suggested."

Julian bristled.

The Galactic Government just looked confused.

Cassie gave me a look, shaking her head and stifling a laugh.

I shrugged. If there was a chance I was going to die the next day, I needed to have a little fun. Besides, I was tired of all the lies and secrets.

The rest of the conversation was pretty boring. We went through troop movements, contingency plans, supplies and tactics, and then more backup plans.

I was falling asleep in my chair before it was all over. All I needed to know was that I would be at the front when the fighting started, supported by the other pack members as well as Commander Shaw and his mechs.

The Order and Galactic Government would have the bulk of their forces in the sky.

Cryx somehow anticipated our needs and had caf brought in for us. I knew it was her because the praetorian handing out the caf delivered mine with a note on it: DON'T FALL ASLEEP IN YOUR MEETING.

I had to grin at that one. In a short time, Cryx had turned from a stem head into someone who was actually trying to better herself. I knew she'd make it. She had a good heart. Sometimes not giving up on the battle was as important as winning it altogether.

I didn't know what time it was when the last detail was ironed out, but it was late. After goodbyes, I found myself heading back to the Immortal Corp tent with Butch at my side.

She fared just about as well as I had in the meeting. With a few yawns, struggling to keep her eyes open.

"I feel you," I told her, scratching her soft ears as we made our way through the camp. "We're almost there. One more fight and then we can do away with all the bureaucracy and long meetings."

"Don't speak too soon," Cassie's familiar voice rang out behind me. "You looked good at the head of the table. And you know how to ruffle a few feathers."

"Who, me?" I asked with a smile and slowed my gait to wait for her. "I'm sure I don't know what you mean, Miss—actually, I don't know your last name."

"It's Evans," Cassie said, coming up to me on the other side of Butch and petting the back of her head.

Butch leaned into the strokes. "If you tell anyone that, I'll have to kill you."

"Your secret's safe with me," I said, crossing my chest. It was getting late and with the lack of sleep, I felt a little goofy. "Where are you going to be when the fighting starts?"

"I'm no pilot." Cassie shrugged. "I'll be on the ground."

The canopy of stars overhead and Mars' twin moons reflecting caught her in a brilliant way. Maybe it was because I didn't have time to notice it before or I refused to, but she was beautiful. Not in a classic sense but in a very lethal sense.

"Why are you looking at me like that?" Cassie asked with a raised eyebrow. "Do I have something on my face?"

"No, no, you're good," I answered as we reached the entrance to my tent. "Well, this is me."

"If I don't see you before it all starts, watch yourself out there," Cassie said. "It would be a shame if we lost you."

"I'm not that easy to kill," I assured her, not sure what to do in that moment. A handshake didn't seem appropriate; a hug definitely wasn't right. "I'll see you again."

"I'm counting on it," Cassie answered with an amused twist of her lips as if she could sense my awkwardness.

If I had known the hell that waited for me on the other side of the night, I would have gone in for the hug.

# NINE

SLEEP CAME EASIER than it should have. With a war about to break and thousands of lives possibly lost the next day, I felt guilty for falling asleep so easily. Maybe that same guilt was what brought on the nightmares.

I stood on the frontline of our army, a red sandy ocean extended in front of me until it ended, enveloped by the Voy. They stood no more than a kilometer out. The hot sun beat down on human and alien alike.

No sound whatsoever broke our standoff. They were a myriad of arms and eyes. I could practically feel hope seeping out of my soul as I counted their numbers.

A glance to my right and left told me we wouldn't live to see the end of the day. We had vastly underestimated their force. There had to be hundreds of thousands of them. There was no way for my brain to do the math, but I imagined there could even be a million.

Fear seized my heart and its good friend panic twisted my gut.

"There's no way we can win this." Cryx appeared by my side. "We're already dead."

I turned to look at her to see a walking corpse. She had a laceration across her neck that made me wonder how her head stayed on at all. Blood dripped down her shirt. Her left eye was gone altogether, revealing a hole inside her head.

"We're all already dead," the army of warriors behind me repeated.

I took a look at every one of them. Cassie, Echo, Preacher, Cage—they were all there. Each one of them wore life-threatening wounds, as if the battle had already happened and they had died. It was their reanimated corpses brought back to issue the warning.

Even the giant Phoenix mech warriors that towered on either side of our flanks were burning and smoking as if they had been through hell themselves.

I clenched my jaw. A sick feeling slid over my stomach. I thought I would vomit in the midst of the death and decay around me.

"You didn't do enough," Madam Eternal accused, pushing her way through the crowd. She was ripped open like the rest. Her right arm hung off her torso by a cord of sinew. "You should have opened the book. Why didn't you open the book? I told you to open the book!"

She screamed at me like a woman possessed.

I tried to swallow, but my mouth was dry. On every side, the bodies pushed around me, asking me why I didn't do more.

"You should have saved us," Sam yelled.

"You could have done more," Julian shouted.

"You weren't enough," Cryx screeched.

They pressed in on me from all sides.

"Daniel!" the first familiar voice directed toward me not full of hate called out. It was X. "Daniel, wake up! This is a dream!"

I struggled against the corpses around me. They all reached for me, trying to pull me down. I searched for X, finally seeing her fighting through the crowd toward my direction.

*This is a nightmare,* I told myself. *This is only a nightmare. I can control my nightmares.*

I looked down at my belt, concentrating on my weapons. Sure enough, they were there. I grabbed my axe and knife and began to fight my way free of the crush of bodies.

I sliced and stabbed my way through friends who looked like they'd already experienced death. I knew it wasn't really them. This was in my head and that was it.

"Over here, Daniel," X cried out. "Over here, you've almost made it. Keep going!"

I couldn't see X through the throng now, but I could

hear her voice as loud and clear as anything. Slicing with my axe as if I were mowing down young trees, I found her.

When I reached her, I didn't see what I had expected.

X was on her knees, her blue synth suit covered in blood. Butch lay dead in her lap. Blood soaked the ground.

"You were too late, Daniel." X looked up at me, tears streaming down her face. "You were too late to save her. You weren't enough to save anyone."

I sat bolt upright in my bed, panting hard.

Butch, who had taken a sleeping position beside my bed, lifted her head to see if I was all right.

A cold sweat fell from my brow while another one soaked my back.

"Daniel, are you okay?" X asked in my head. "Your heart rate is through the roof. I was monitoring your sleep and about to wake you up."

"Just a bad dream," I wheezed. "I'll live."

The light sounds of footfalls and people talking wafted through the curtain wall of my tent. A glow could be seen through the fabric.

"Is it time?" I asked.

"It is," X confirmed. "The Voy have not made any movements yet, but others all around the camp are opening comm channels and preparing for the day."

"We should, too," I said, swinging my feet out of

the bed then leaning down to pet Butch. The massive wolf smiled kindly at me and shoved the side of her head harder against my hand.

"I'm glad you're not dead," I whispered, stroking her head and back.

"Daniel," X sounded worried. "Are you sure you're okay?"

"Define 'okay,'" I replied, standing to stretch. "We're hours away from battling aliens for the fate of humankind."

"Poor choice of words on my end." X stifled a chuckle. "Are you in the right mindset for this?"

"I have to be," I said, throwing on my pants and boots. "I—"

Sirens exploded all over the encampment.

"X?" I asked as Butch jumped to her feet. Other members of the Pack Protocol were waking now and asking what was going on.

"Chatter on the comm line indicates the Voy are on the move," X rattled off. "Patching you into a comm line with Wesley and Colonel Strife now."

"I'll coordinate with Julian and get our forces in the air," Colonel Strife was saying. "Daniel, good to have you. You ready to go to work, son?"

"I'm ready," I lied, still zipping up my pants. "Where do you want me?"

"Good to hear you," Wesley answered. I could hear the excitement in his voice. Not anxious or worried but full of energy and primed for the moment. "Gear up with your team at the staging area, then rendezvous with Commander Shaw and his mech corps to head out."

"Understood," I acknowledged, not knowing where either my gear or the staging area was but relying on X to show me the way.

X never let me down. Without a word, a map of the area popped up in a square box in the lower right hand corner of my vision.

I heard someone howling in the tent. I lifted back the fabric flap to my own small section, barely large enough for a cot and Butch to lie down.

Jax was in the middle of the room with his head lifted to the tent ceiling. His thick beard and bare muscular torso made him look like some kind of werewolf.

Echo came from his tent, howling as well as he jumped up and down on his toes, mentally preparing himself for what came next.

Sam and Angel pulled back the drapes from their sleeping quarters, the former rolling her eyes, the latter looking pissed that she had been woken from her sleep. Angel's dark hair was a mess; a line of drool still fell from the corner of her mouth.

"For the love of all that is holy, is the howling really necessary?" Angel chided, rubbing her eyes.

"Tradition is tradition," Preacher stated as the last

member of the pack to join us exited his sleeping area. He hobbled on an ornate cane with a carved wolf head for the handle. "You used to howl with them."

"Yeah, I used to do a lot of things, but I'm not eighteen anymore," Angel grumbled, finally opening her eyes.

Butch joined in with Jax and Echo a second later. I couldn't help myself.

I tilted my head back and let out a howl myself. I understood the psychology behind posturing and creating noise for battle. Everyone, whether they admitted it or not, was nervous. Movement and sound helped us to expel some of that energy as well as pose a dominating stance over the fear that sought to take us.

Sam and Preacher answered, joining our call.

Angel gave me a deadpan stare. "You all are children."

"Come on, Archangel," Sam teased. "One more time. For old time's sake. Who knows when we're going to run together again?"

"I hate you," Angel said, finally cracking a grin before she lifted her head toward the ceiling and ripped an animalist howl.

"There we go!" Jax shouted, slapping his hands together.

"What in the name of the Voy is going on in here?" Cryx asked, exiting her section of the tent. "And I'm the child."

We all laughed as we raided the food in the middle of the room on our way out of the tent.

"The battlefield isn't going to be any place for you," I said, taking a knee next to Butch. "You stay here with Cryx and keep each other safe."

Butch looked at me with ears perked up straight. I stared into those big yellow eyes of hers and I swore she could understand me. There was more there than just the pupils of an animal.

I wondered if, when Rose resurrected the species, she added more to their DNA, somehow increasing their intelligence. An answer to that would have to wait.

I rose to my feet and nodded at Cryx.

"Anything goes bad, you and Brother Enoch head back to Dragon Hold ASAP," I instructed. "Bapz will be able to lock down the place and I'm sure he'll have an exit plan off Mars."

"You're going to be fine," Cryx insisted, unexpectedly rushing to me. She slammed her body into mine and gave me a fierce hug that took my breath away. "You're going to be fine. Come back; you have a lot to teach me about fighting."

I wasn't really the hugging type, but right now, I couldn't help but give her a squeeze back. She still felt small. She was a young woman but still a kid in my eyes.

"I'll be back," I told her. Then, not knowing what

came over me, I broke the embrace and looked her in the eye. "I'm proud of the woman you're becoming. You keep fighting to be that woman. You were meant for great things."

We both stood there shocked.

Tears welled in her eyes as she nodded.

I left before I could shed tears of my own. Freaking kids brought out the best in me for some reason. I was uncomfortable with that. I hurried out of the tent, following the pack to gear up and do what I was created to do.

Before the day was over, a single species would stand victorious.

# TEN

THE TENT where we geared up was actually right next to the area we were to rendezvous with Commander Shaw.

Flat black ceramic armor was provided for us along with helmets and weapons of our choice. I took a heavy repeater that looked like something the GG would use.

Preacher rattled off the gear we donned as if he were reading from a manual. The guy knew a lot about weapons and gear.

"The armor will stop any lightweight rounds as well as shrapnel. As long as you don't get a direct hit from something large, you'll be good to go. It won't feel pretty, though." Preacher gingerly put on his armor, still careful with his wounds. "We have our own weapons here along with a variety of heavier firepower courtesy of our friends at the GG. Whatever our differences, I'll say this for our boys in yellow, they like their weapons."

"Hey, you think we should tell the old man to sit this one out?" Jax asked as I holstered my MK II and clipped a few extra drums for it to my magnetic belt. "I mean, he doesn't heal like us anymore and he's still limping."

I looked over at Preacher, who was helping Echo strap into his chest armor.

"You think anything we're going to say to him is going to stop him?" I asked, putting on the steel wrist-bands that would act to recall my axe and knife once thrown. "I mean, if someone told you or me to stay back right now, would we?"

"Good point," Jax conceded, adjusting something that looked like a rocket launcher on his back. "Hey, looks like you have company."

I followed Jax's line of sight to the entrance of the tent. Cassie walked toward us. She wore a tight-fitting black bodysuit with the Order emblem of the red cross on her left shoulder.

"Your team have room for one more?" Cassie directed the question at me but looked at all of us in turn. "Julian wants someone to coordinate on the ground, and well, I couldn't think of a better unit to team up with."

"A Cyber Hunter in the pack?" Angel pursed her

lips. "I don't know, our upstanding reputation might get called into question."

"I think we have room for one more." Preacher looked at me with his one good eye for consensus. "What do you think?"

"Can she howl?" I asked Cassie.

"Oh, good question," Jax added.

"Can I what?" Cassie sputtered incredulously.

"Can you howl?" I repeated, throwing my head back and letting out a long wail. "Like that."

"Are you serious right now?" Cassie placed her hands on her curvy hips. "We're about to go bleed together on the sands of Mars and you're asking me if I can howl?"

"I don't think she can howl," Echo teased her.

"Just do it. They're not going to let it go," Sam counseled her.

Cassie looked up and ripped a howl that would have made Butch proud.

I walked over to her and extended a hand.

"Welcome to the pack, Cyber Hunter," I said. "Pay's not that great, we're probably going to get shot at a lot, and I don't really know how we accrue vacation days. My memory isn't so good."

"Two weeks of vacation a year," Angel chimed in, throwing up both hands, palms up. "I know, it's a crime."

"The Voy aren't breaking their forces; they're

heading straight for Athens like we suspected," Wesley spoke into my ear. "We have a better count on them now—somewhere around a hundred thousand ground vehicles with twice that many in the air and at least a dozen of those bug creatures. They're bigger than the one we faced at the Way settlement. A lot bigger."

Images flashed across my vision with X's aid as Wesley listed off the facts. The Voy were approaching in a cloud of red sand. The sky was nearly blotted out by the level of air support with them.

Alien vehicles that crawled more than rolled hovered over the sandy ground came in waves. They looked like big brown tubes more than anything else.

"We're already in the air," Colonel Strife reported. "ETA to when the Voy will engage with ground forces?"

"Ground forces are departing now," Wesley answered. "Two hours and twenty-one minutes until contact. Daniel, open up a line with Commander Shaw so you make sure you don't miss your ride."

"Got it," I responded. "We're geared up and ready to roll out."

I waved over to the rest of the unit. Everyone besides Cassie was ready to go. She quickly placed her body armor and helmet on.

"X," I asked. "Can we get a line with Commander Shaw?"

"Opening now," X said as something like a roar of thrusters sounded just outside our tent.

"Daniel, are you there?" Commander Shaw asked. "We're about to lift off."

"We're coming," I said and gestured for the pack to exit the tent.

The team grabbed last-minute charge packs and weapons before joining me. The sounds of thrusters were getting louder and louder as more engines were fired up.

When we exited the rear of the tent, an airfield greeted us with soldiers from all types of corporations filing into square containers.

Each container held a series of seats like the inside of a dropship. When the container was closed, a carrier support ship would hover over it, clamp down on the container holding the soldiers, and fly off.

"Not the sexiest way to travel, but it gets the job done," Captain Zoe Valentine yelled over the sound of the crafts. She jogged over to us, wearing her mustard-colored praetorian armor. "You ready to go?"

"We're ready," I confirmed just as loudly over the sounds of the crate crafts in the air. "I didn't know you were going to be with us."

Zoe motioned for me to follow her to a crate on the left reserved for us. She entered first.

Inside the crate, four rows of harnesses were lined up, two against either wall, then the other two rows back to back in the center.

The harnesses were set up in a way that let us stand

and strap in rather than sit. The harnesses themselves were black but everything else in the craft was white.

Windows lined the walls much like a dropship to afford us a look out.

The harnesses were set in lines of ten, allowing forty soldiers to be carried by the Crate Craft at once. We piled in, taking the rows on the left corner. Behind us, a group of Galactic Government praetorians filed in.

I could tell they were looking at us by how quiet they were.

I strapped in, harnessing myself in place by the shoulder and chest. The far side of the crate also had a pair of double doors that would slide out, allowing us to disembark from each end in a hurry if the occasion so called.

The harness felt snug, clipping under my arms to keep me upright and prevent me from falling. Cassie was on my left and Jax on my right. Zoe stood across from me.

The praetorian captain craned her neck forward to address the other soldiers filing into the crate.

"You prats ready to bring some pain!"

"Arooh!" the praetorians answered as one.

I reached down to my helmet clipped to my magnetic belt. I maneuvered it around the harness at my chest and slammed it down on my head. The clear visor was equipped with a HUD that I didn't really need since I had X, but was nice nonetheless.

The HUD gave me a readout when I turned to look at different individuals. It also showed a map of the area in the lower left corner as well as a scrolling dialogue bar at the bottom of my visor.

"I'm loaded with Daniel and his team and ready to go," Zoe said on the line we shared with Commander Shaw. "We're in Crate ten, seven, five, one."

"Understood, securing the crate and preparing to lift," Commander Shaw responded. "I'll see you on the ground. Godspeed."

My mouth was dry and I had to poop. Whenever I got really excited or nervous, I had a bad case of the runs. I'd like to think it happened to the best of us.

"Well, would you look at us, X," I said into my helmet. "The moon, Earth, and now Mars. Listen, I don't know what happens to you if I die, but if you want out now, all you have to do is ask. I can disconnect the implant before this all start—"

"I can't believe you'd even ask me that." X sounded offended. "Besides, if you die, I'll be fine. You just worry about doing what you have to, to survive. I'll help where I can but give you space to work."

"You're the best," I told her.

"I know," she answered.

I could picture her smiling as she said the words.

Memories of my nightmare from the previous night flooded through my brain like the Voy cascading over a sand dune. I saw them all again. I saw all the dead faces of everyone in this crate.

*You can't let them down,* I thought to myself. *Whatever you have to do. Whatever it takes. You can't let them down.*

"Craft locking on to the crate in three," a voice said over the comms unit inside the crate.

Red warning lights flashed inside the holding box.

"Two," the female voice counted down. "One."

The box shuddered as the ship made contact and locked on to us. A second later, thrusters fired and we were lifted from the ground.

I was so glad I didn't get space sick anymore as we were hoisted into the air and then forward. It seemed I wasn't the only one who suffered from a serious bout with space sickness.

One of the praetorians vomited in his helmet across the way.

"Ewww, that's so sick!" his praetorian brothers and sisters teased him.

"Clean up on aisle one," someone shouted amongst the good-natured jeers and jokes.

"It's going to be a short ride," Wesley's voice explained over the comms. "We're having to set you down and prepare the defensive line earlier than expected. The Voy have increased their speed."

"What about the World Engine?" I asked. "If they've committed their forces to us right now, what about hitting them with that?"

"It's good for a single shot, don't forget," Julian sounded over the comms. "With that said, I agree with Daniel. We set up our lines then decimate as many of them as possible before they reach us."

"No argument there," Colonel Strife agreed.

"Then that's the plan," I said inside my helmet. "We set our lines then deploy the World Engine. Whatever's left of their forces, we'll clean up."

"Contact, we have contact!" Colonel Strife screamed out of nowhere.

Explosions ripped through the air around us as dark laser beams rained down from the sky.

Our ship shuddered. People began screaming and yelling all around us.

"What's happening out there?" Wesley asked for all of us.

"Voy ships came out of nowhere, cloaking technology or something else, maybe," Julian answered over the comms.

"Give us some cover!" Commander Shaw shouted. "My crate crafts are easy targets."

"Moving in now!" Julian answered.

"We're here," Colonel Strife added.

I never felt so useless in my life. Here I was strapped to a harness inside a steel box praying that I'd live to take out my vengeance on the Voy.

# ELEVEN

BESIDES THE COMM line that was going crazy with Colonel Strife, Julian, and Commander Shaw coordinating a defense, I had only the windows to see what was going on.

The small ball-shaped fighter ships of the Voy zipped in and out of the windows' view. The craft shuddered from the impact and tossed and turned as the pilot tried to keep us steady.

"God please help us!" A praetorian screamed from somewhere in his harness.

Someone else was screaming, another laughing like a mad woman.

"Hold it together!" Zoe shouted through gritted teeth.

"Voy attacking from above were cloaked until the very last minute." Julian finally gave us an answer to what was going on. "We didn't have a clue their ships were there."

"Just get us on the ground," I growled. "X, how long until we reach the—"

An explosion rocked the Crate Craft we were inside so violently, I swear my intestines were shaken. The ship trembled and rolled. Black smoke blew from one of the engines.

"Brace for impact!" the pilot bellowed amongst the screams of those inside. "We're going down!"

The next few seconds, I tried not to throw up as we plummeted toward the ground below. My senses were working on overdrive. People were yelling as more explosions ripped through the sky around us, and then impact.

I'm not sure what kind of training the pilot had gone through, but despite the hit and damage to the ship, she landed the craft intact. We struck the ground right side up so hard, I thought I might have broken my ankles.

The chest rigs around us actually helped with that, absorbing the blow from the ground and lifting upward a bit to compensate for the pressure.

I looked to my right and left at the others who were as surprised as I was. I don't think anyone expected to land in one piece.

"Let's go, let's go, let's go!" Captain Valentine

ordered as our chest harnesses unclipped on their own. Both sets of doors opened. "Weapons ready!"

I filed out of the crate with the rest of my unit and Captain Valentine's praetorians.

The desert around us was a living nightmare. The sky was alive with those circular alien fighters battling the much larger Order and Galactic Government ships.

A dozen Crate Crafts carrying soldiers had crashed in various states of destruction. Some were totally destroyed while others had survivors struggling to free themselves from the metal container before the entire ship blew apart.

"Let's help who we can!" I shouted, running to the nearest downed Crate Craft that lay burning on its left side. "X, how much farther to the staging ground?"

"We were still a few kilometers out," X answered.

I needed to say more, but right now, I had larger issues to solve. The Crate Craft in front of me was a coffin. One side had been smashed on impact. The other side's door was open a crack, just enough for those inside screaming for help to get their hands out but no more.

Bodies piled behind the doors, begging for aid.

"The ship's leaking fluid," X warned in my head. "Probability that it'll explode in the next few minutes is high."

"Come on here; give me a hand!" I roared to anyone that would listen. I shoved my finger into the gap between the doors and tore at it with every ounce of strength I had in my arms. "Rawww!"

"Help us!" The screams from within fought against one another to be heard.

"Open the doors!" another voice desperately implored.

Jax appeared across from me along with Echo and Cassie. Sam and Angel popped up on either side of me, all gripping the edge of the doors.

We tore at the door. It gave an inch. I put my back into it, spurred on by the screams of those inside. It gave, maybe the slightest bit, maybe that was my imagination.

"Together," I instructed the team as Zoe and Preacher made it to the door. Preacher shoved his cane in the space between the open doors. "On three, everything you got and don't stop till this son of a crip opens!"

Heads nodded.

"One, two, three!" I counted down in a hurry. In the back of my mind was X's warning. This thing was primed to go up in a ball of flames.

In that moment the GG, Immortal Corp, and the Order all worked together. My fingers cramped. Despite my gloves, my hands still trembled with pain as the edge of the door bore into my skin.

I couldn't help it any more than a sneeze that refused to die. I roared along with the others, my feet fighting for traction as the muscles in my hands screamed their own cries of agony.

Defeat was never an option, not for myself or for those inside. That door was going to open; there was no other option.

A moment later, the doors finally gave. Something like the sound of a piece of metal snapping inside the door-locking mechanism met our ears. Our combined super-human strength was more than even steel could handle.

The doors slammed open and the trapped praetorians inside ran out like their lives depended on it. There was no time for thanks. The fight in the sky had lessened now, but there were still crafts plummeting to the sandy ground all around us.

"Hurry, hurry!" Preacher encouraged everyone out of the now opened doors of the crate.

Those injured in the crash were aided by those able to walk. We had the entire crate cleared in under a minute. Good thing, too. A fire broke out inside the crate just as the last praetorian cleared the doors. They would have been cooked alive.

"We need to get clear," Cassie shouted over the sounds of battle. "It's going to blow!"

We took her advice, sprinting away from the ship.

She was right.

We hadn't made it more than a few meters when a

concussive explosion slammed into my back. It wasn't enough to send me flying, but I stumbled in the sand.

I looked to my right and left to make sure we had all made it clear. The only person to get thrown at all was Preacher. Human and still not completely recovered, he moved slower than any of us.

Refusing to stay down, Preacher turned his fall into a roll and popped back onto his feet with a limp.

"We've got them on the run," Julian said over the comms. "I don't think they wanted to do more here than harass us. They're retreating now."

"We've got a bulk of wounded here," I answered. "We'll carry the wounded and press forward. Is there any way you can have the frontline move back and meet us halfway?"

"I'm already en route to you," Commander Shaw advised. "We'll be there in a few minutes. Just stay put and care for the wounded. We'll start coordinating medic crates to take the wounded back."

The next minutes were spent doing what we could for those in pain. The praetorian medics took care of their own while the rest of us put out fires and secured what weapons we could from the downed crafts.

I saw a plume of dust rising over a sand dune. It was in the direction Commander Shaw would be heading from. I jogged across the sand up toward the dune. Anyone who's tried to run up a dune will tell you it sucks. Full armor and weapons make it suck that much more.

I crested the top, looking out to see a scene that both inspired and horrified me. Commander Shaw was retreating toward us with an army of mech warriors painted in the reds and whites of the Phoenix corporation.

Each mech carried a section of a cement barrier designed to give ground troops cover. They hefted the heavy pieces of our defenses over their shoulders like steel workers carrying heavy tools.

Along with them were a series of support and troop transport hover tanks. The tanks carried the combined soldiers of the various corporations that came to defend humanity.

I saw their sigils painted on tanks and worn proudly on soldiers. The Yakuza, the Overlords, Valkyrie Industries, Apex; they were all there.

That part inspired me.

The part that horrified me was a massive rolling plume of sand that came behind them. Thanks to the HUD in my helmet and my own advanced sight abilities, I was barely able to make out what looked like a sandstorm.

A wall of red racing toward us that at this distance seemed safe, but I knew better.

"Is everyone seeing what I'm seeing?" I asked into the shared comm line. "We have trouble."

"I see it," Commander Shaw answered. "We'll make it to you before they catch us, but maybe it's time for the World Engine?"

"Wesley?" I asked.

"Julian, Colonel Strife, if you're ready, I agree with Daniel and the commander," Wesley answered. "It's time."

"You've got my blessing," Colonel Strife stated. "Kill them all."

"If we hit the rear of their mass now, then we'll avoid any damage to our own lines," Julian answered. "Shaw, if you can get those defenses in place that'll be added protection for our forces."

"Launch now; we're nearly there," Commander Shaw shouted over the noise on his end of the comms that sounded like gears and levers turning. "Daniel, get your unit behind the defensive line as soon as we place it."

"Roger," I said, already moving back down the dune. The first line of mech warriors running across the desert carrying the cement structures were already passing my location.

The massive mountains of steel placed the thick barrier on the ground between two giant dunes, each one hitting the ground with a resounding boom. The logs of cement had to be a full meter thick and as high as my chest.

The mechs under Commander Shaw's expert leadership placed the barrier between and up to the pair of dunes, creating a pair of towers. The vehicles stormed through in an opening one of the mechs made by lifting a barrier up like a gate.

"X, can you link me to the pack, Cassie and Zoe?" I asked, running toward the area that would act as our new defensive lines.

"Done," X responded so fast, I knew she must have been anticipating my request.

*Man, I really need to give X a raise or do something nice for her if we live through this*, I thought to myself. *What do you get an AI?*

"We need to get the wounded to the rear of our line, where they'll be crated back to the staging ground," I commanded, instead of worrying what to get X. "World Engine is about to fire. We need to get everyone on the defensive line down ASAP."

"On it," Zoe answered. "I'll have my praetorians get the wounded to the rear.

"We'll work with Commander Shaw to get everyone in position and behind cover," Preacher said through a grunt of pain.

I caught sight of him limping with his cane to the newly erected lines. He walked with a tight hitch in his gait. I could only imagine the level of pain and discomfort he was in. More than that, having to deal with one's body not healing as quickly as you were used to had to be disturbing and strange.

"We got it," Echo chimed in. "You can count on us."

Everyone worked together. Zoe moved the wounded to the rear where the Crate Crafts coordinated with one another, lifting the wounded back to safety.

Commander Shaw, maneuvered the rest of the barriers in place with the help of his mech unit. Turrets had been placed on top of the dunes that acted as organic watchtowers of death.

What's more, many of the vehicles the mercenary corporations drove also supported heavy weapons. These were maneuvered behind the barriers as well.

Thousands of soldiers stood ready. I took up position on the right dune tower next to the turret. Commander Shaw took the left dune.

The approaching sandstorm made by the sheer number of our enemy was clearer now. I still couldn't make out individual soldiers, but I knew they were coming.

"You ready for this?" Cassie asked, appearing at my side. "If the World Engine doesn't take them all, we're the line that has to hold them."

"We will," I answered, feeling resolve mold my words. "We have to. They get through us, they have a straight run at the staging ground, then Athens."

A rogue thought crossed my mind. I remembered Sam telling me that Papa and the Reapers would be coming to lend aid.

"Any word on help coming from the gangs on

Earth?" I asked into the comms to anyone who had an answer.

"Last report I saw was that they were too far out," Commander Shaw answered. "Like the bulk of the GG forces, they'd get here tonight when the fighting's over."

"World Engine is primed and ready to fire." Julian ended that conversation with his statement. "Hold on to something. Here we go."

# TWELVE

"WORLD ENGINE FIRING IN FIVE, FOUR..." Julian began the countdown.

I looked to my right and left. The Pack surrounded me with their weapons ready. We pressed our bodies against the heavy cement bricks in front of us with our chests, shoulders, and heads exposed.

The massive turret on my right was manned by a member of the Valkyrie Corporation. She looked at me and nodded in a silent act of strength.

"Three, two," Julian continued in a steady voice.

I nodded back. My heart picked up in tempo as I directed my eyes forward. Using the zoom feature in my HUD and my own enhanced vision, thanks to X, I had a great view.

"One," Julian finally said. "Fire."

A fleeting thought of remorse touched my heart. We were about to end thousands of lives. The moment was there and gone like a mist in the middle of the hot desert. It was them or us. That was the simple truth and I sure as heck wasn't going to let it be us. Not on my watch, not while I still drew breath.

"World Engine has fired," Julian reported. "Impact in two, one."

If Julian said zero, I couldn't tell. The sound was nothing like I had ever heard. When the steel rod touched down, it was as if it sucked all the sound into it for a moment before expelling a noise like Mars cracking.

The rolling red sandstorm coming toward us expanded outward at breakneck speed. One second we were looking at the sandstorm, the next the ground shook. Our ears were assailed with the sound of impact and a concussive blast tore through us.

I hit the ground, taking shelter behind the cement barricade with everyone else on the line. Wind slammed past the barricade in a gale of angry fury.

Chatter was alive in my comms, but I couldn't hear what was being said.

A second later, the howling wind died away. I looked around to make sure everyone was all right. Jax gave me a thumbs-up. Sam nodded along with everyone else.

I could hear again.

"Direct hit where we wanted it to land," Wesley reported. "We hit them right at the rear of their numbers."

"I can't imagine much lived through that," Colonel Strife grunted. "Good work, gentlemen."

All around us, cheers were going up from the defenders.

*Did we do it?* I asked myself as I looked over the cement barricade. *Could it really be that easy?*

I scanned the area in front of me, trying to see past the debris and clouds of sand. It was impossible at the moment, even with my enhanced vision.

The cheering of all those around didn't touch the mercenaries around me. The pack along with Cassie knew better. No fight was that easy. The leaders on the comms likewise reserved their celebratory congratulations.

"Yes! Eat it, you four-armed, six-eyed alien scum!" the soldier on the turret called down to us from our right. She swiveled in her seat, taking us in. "Why aren't you celebrating? We killed them! We just ended the war before it even started. We'll teach any alien who wants to mess with us to think twice."

I ignored her for the time being not because she was pissing me off, although that was some of it. There was something off. That truth came not from what I could see but a deep instinctual feeling that lived somewhere in my gut.

"This is all wrong," I finally said out loud more to myself than anyone else. "Something's wrong."

"What are you talking about?" The Valkyrie warrior threw up her hands toward the air in front of us. "We just annihilated their entire army!"

"Daniel's right," Colonel Strife sounded in my ear. "I'm going to do a fly over closer to the impact. Voy fighter crafts have pulled back—to where—I'm not sure."

"Understood," Wesley answered.

"Feeding visuals to you now," Colonel Strife said. Somewhere overhead, a ship moved forward. A screen popped to life in my helmet showing me a bird's eye view of the ground below.

The dust was still thick but less now so we could make out small unmoving pieces of body and corpses on the ground. We had hit them. We had hit them hard enough to decimate the Voy force in front of us.

Still, something wasn't right. Then it struck me like a thunderbolt.

"Their bugs, those big bugs they breed for war," I said. "They're not there. Where are the bugs?"

I scanned the images coming through again. Sure enough, nothing of the wreckage was even remotely large enough to be the giant insects we planned on engaging. There were sections of Voy vehicles and bodies but no bugs.

"When that bug attacked us at the Way station, it came from underground," Colonel Strife answered. "Did they burrow down?"

This had always been a possibility, but one we were prepared to deal with, with the help of Commander Shaw's mech. There was no way to prepare for an attack like that except for when it came.

"Could they have burrowed down to avoid the blast?" Wesley asked.

"We still would have got them," Julian answered, knowing the blast penetrated the surface of the planet. "Unless…"

Julian's voice trailed off.

"Unless what?" I asked, not really wanting an answer.

"Unless that was only a portion of their forces sent out to make us use our weapons," Julian answered in a quiet voice.

"We have movement from their base." Wesley's tone said it all. Something was wrong. "Using the same high density scanners we can make out their heat signatures through their barrier. Julian's right there are more—a lot more coming fast."

Wesley gave us access to see what he was viewing. An aerial shot showed up in a screen inside my HUD.

To his credit, the man kept it together rather well. The Voy's camp was unloading with a horde of Voy soldiers.

Massive winged bug creatures larger than the one that attacked at the Way settlement carried platforms packed with Voy soldiers.

The alien bugs flew just over the ground on their way toward us. It was impossible to tell how fast they were coming, but I could guess they weren't wasting any time.

They had to be two stories tall with bodies armored and segmented. Their wings opened up on either side of their bodies like a flying beetle's more than a moth's. I wasn't sure what was more horrifying, the sight of the creatures or the sheer number of them.

Hundreds of the giant insects carried thousands of Voy soldiers on the flat platforms.

"Nothing's changed," Colonel Strife asserted. "Here we go. This is what we expected. Get your soldiers in the right mindset. At the speed they're traveling, I'm showing fifteen minutes until they arrive."

I swallowed hard, not able to muster enough saliva to do the act justice. Celebratory calls and cheers still echoed around me. They had no idea what was coming for them. A force ten times the one that had been heading for us was on its way.

"Then they did sacrifice ten maybe twenty percent of their number just to see how we would counterattack," X thought out loud. "They willingly killed them."

"World Engine is down not that it makes much of a difference now," Julian answered us all. "Voy fighter ships took to the atmosphere and blew it to pieces."

"Colonel Strife is right," Wesley said. "All group leaders. Get your people ready to fight and give them hell."

"I'm not really a people person," I said to X. "But here we go."

I jumped on top of the turret next to the Valkyrie officer. I lifted my MK II from its holster, pointing the barrel into the air and toward the oncoming Voy no one could see yet. I fired a round.

That was enough to get everyone within hearing distance looking toward me.

"X, this helmet have external speakers?" I asked. "I need them to hear me."

"Yes, they're set inside the collar of your armor," X answered. "You're on."

I looked down at all of them. From the Pack members to the praetorians and those from the other corporation, everyone on my sand dune looked at me. I could tell Commander Shaw was doing something similar on his dune. The cheers and laughs had quieted. Everyone sensed all was not well.

"Take off your helmets," I started. "I want to look in your eyes."

I removed my own, running a gloved hand through my short dark hair.

Some were slower than others, but everyone complied. Confusion was clear on many of their faces, the death of joy visible on others as they realized this fight was far from over.

"Some of you know me." I began shouting the words to be heard by as many of those gathered as possible. "Many of you don't. All that matters right now is that you know I'm your brother and I'm going to fight with you with everything I've got. The Voy you saw decimated by the World Engine were only a fraction of the enemy force. The rest of the Voy army is on its way now. They'll be here in fifteen minutes."

Shocked expressions from most rippled through the crowd. Many looked at one another for answers no one had.

"The World Engine was a one-shot weapon," I continued. "It's up to us now. Every single one of you give me everything you've got and it will be enough! Together, we'll break their will to fight! Everything you've got for the person standing next to you and we'll be the last species standing today!"

I saw the change happen in front of me. Each one of these men and women were trained to fight. Many of them already had in previous encounters whether they be praetorian for the GG or private muscle for one of the corporations.

I hopped off the turret, looking at my own pack members, who stood with their helmets in the crooks of their elbows.

"I need you all to spread out up and down the line on our side of the dune," I told them. "Every sort of heavy weapon you can find should be on the barrier and enough ammunition to last us all day and night if need be."

"We got you," Echo said, already turning to obey with the others.

"Good speech by the way," Angel said with a wink. "I didn't think you had it in you. The Daniel I knew hated public speaking."

I headed down our side of the dune as everyone moved to fulfill orders. The nervous buzz was back in the air as soldiers steeled their resolve for the chaos that would come next.

Ammunition depots were set behind my dune and Commander Shaw's. Right now, our lines looked like a semi-circle. Our two dunes were in the middle with the open valley in between. On our flanks were the mech units to make sure no one got behind our back.

The ammunition depot was just a fancy word for a series of supply tents with crates of rounds for various heavy weapons. I was about to grab one and lug it up the side of the sand dune, when a familiar voice caught my attention.

"That was a stirring speech. It's exactly what they

needed to hear," Madam Eternal said. "Well done, Daniel Hunt."

I looked over to see the woman still dressed in her crimson red robe. Despite the circumstances we found ourselves in, she carried a steady smile on her full lips. More than that, she carried the ancient book we had picked up from Mordred in her hands.

# THIRTEEN

I GAVE HER A PARENTAL STARE, which was ironic in and of itself because she was older than me. At least I thought she was. There was no telling what kind of tricks this woman had up her wide robe sleeves.

"Are you supposed to be carrying that?" I looked down at the Relic. "Julian would be pissed if he saw you with it. How did you get it anyway? I thought it was back in our tent before we left."

"Yes, well, Julian and the Order had their opportunity and failed." Madam Eternal shrugged while ignoring my latter question altogether. "It will take me time to set up if and when you decide to use it. I've seen the size of the force coming our way. Trust me, we'll need it."

I sighed heavily. All the various agendas everyone had were starting to wear on me.

"We agreed to use it as a last resort, so if that's still the plan, I say go ahead and you do you," I told the woman, looking her up and down. "You might want to put on some armor. Things are about to get chaotic around here."

"Much like you, Daniel, there is more to me than what at first meets the eye," Madam Eternal said with a twinkle in her eye. "I will prepare the Relic then take my place on the frontline. Along with my healing abilities, I have a few tricks up my sleeve for the Voy invaders."

"We need all the help we can get," I answered, jerking my head over to the crates. "If you're heading up to the dune, we're moving ammunition there now."

"With you and Commander Shaw on the dunes, I thought I'd take up the valley between them," Madam Eternal said without hesitation. "Naturally, they'll funnel that way. If your turrets don't stop them, that is."

It wasn't like I was going to talk the woman out of anything. I decided to save my breath and just nod.

Madam Eternal walked away with the Relic under the crook of her elbow.

"That woman is either some kind of genius or bat crip crazy," I said to X. "Maybe both."

"Many geniuses throughout time have been considered neurotic and even a bit eccentric," X observed. "Although Madam Eternal's track record speaks for itself. As one of the corporations, although small in size, it's respected and honored by the others."

"Well, I guess we won't have to wait long to see what she can do," I answered, grabbing a crate of power packs for the heavy turret on the dune and lugging it up the steep sandy slope.

The crate had to weigh eighty maybe even ninety pounds. In full armor with the sun still overhead, it was a lesson in perseverance. I felt like I took a step back every time I placed a foot forward. The way my boots sank into the sand was frustrating to say the least.

"You need a hand?" Cassie asked, coming down the slope to grab more ammunition. "You look pissed."

"Me pissed?" I gave her a fake smile. "No, you must be thinking of someone else."

Cassie came over and lifted the crate of power packs for the turret like it was nothing. Her Cyber Hunter enhancements made her much stronger than I was.

"You were very inspiring," Cassie said as we finished struggling up the dune together. "You missed your calling in life. You should have been a motivational speaker."

"Who knows, there still might be time yet," I said, looking at the Cyber Hunter who was more to me than just a person but a friend. "Once we repel the Voy, I get back to the hold and have X and Bapz help me kick off my career as an author and speaker. I can see it now. My first book will be titled *How I Became a Super Soldier, Lost My Memory, and Saved Humanity*."

Cassie barked a laugh and rolled her eyes. "You're crazy, you know that, right?"

"Naw, truly crazy people don't know they're crazy," I said as we reached the top of the dune and placed the crate alongside the other behind the cement barricade. "Besides, I never claimed to be sane."

"I don't think any of us are," Cassie said, taking in the soldiers all around us mounting weapons on the cement defensive structure. "Maybe a little bit of crazy is okay."

In that moment, I was struck by the humanity we all shared. Yes, we were enhanced, but not immortal. What would happen if I died? What would happen to the Hold, Cryx, Bapz, and Butch, even?

"X," I said, looking at Cassie as I spoke. "I want you to draw up an official document and send it to Bapz that if anything happens to me, the members of the Pack and Cassie are to inherit Dragon Hold."

"Daniel," Cassie said, about to say more.

I cut her off. "You all are the best people for the job. Who knows how many of us are going to make it out of this alive."

"We'll make it," Cassie said with a stone cold face. "We're going to live to see tomorrow. We're going to show the Voy who we are and we'll send a message to the rest of the universe while we're at it. They'll think twice about ever coming to mess with humans."

"I hope you're right, but just in case," I said with a good-natured grin. "You got that, X?"

"Understood," X answered.

"The Voy should be close enough to see with your enhanced sight," Wesley said through the comm channel. "Colonel Strife and Julian, do what you can to intercept the first wave."

"Understood," Colonel Strife answered.

"We'll set up strafing runs and see if we can't pull some of the larger bugs away from the ground forces," Julian added.

I looked to my left over the cement barricade. Sure enough, another wall of red sand was being kicked up in the distance. This sandstorm was different. I could see large black shapes traveling over the sand like dropships.

I knew what they really were. The massive bug creatures the Voy grew in their sick twisted laboratories underground.

"We're getting an incoming transmission broadcasted to all channels," X warned.

I was able to see a screen laid over my vision and hear the broadcast thanks to the chip behind my right ear that connected me to X. Others had to put their helmets on to see and hear who was talking.

An image popped to life in front of me of two Voy standing side by side. I recognized them both. One was taller, wearing a white robe over her feminine body. Her name was Talia. My interaction with her had been brief when I was captured.

The other, shorter and more rotund of the two, was Dall. I felt heat rise to my chest as I took in his smug little face. I was going to kill him not just for what he did to me but for what he had done to Preacher. I was going to make him pay and it wasn't going to be fast either.

I could guess they were still in their fortified base under the camouflaged dome in the side of the mountain. The room they stood in was plain with grey steel equipment I didn't recognize behind them.

"To the defenders on the barricades," Talia spoke in a light friendly manner, "lay down your weapons and allow yourselves to be conscripted into the Voy Empire. There is nothing for you down the path of violence besides death and ruin. You do not need to die today. If you insist on your course of action, we will kill two-thirds of all humanity and enslave the rest."

"You are misguided by your leaders." Dall took up the message of propaganda. "Bend your knee and you will find salvation in a superior and gracious ally. We will hear your answer by the one who leads your forces."

"That's you," Wesley told me on a private channel.

"You sure Shaw or Colonel Strife shouldn't answer them?" I asked, trying to hide the doubt in my voice.

"The coalition of corporations chose you," Wesley reminded me. "Colonel Strife and the GG were late to the party. It's you, Daniel. Be the leader I know you are."

"I can send a returning transmission," X volunteered.

"Do it," I told her, getting my head right. Honestly, I had no idea what I was going to say.

"You're on," X told me.

"To the Voy invaders," I said slowly. "Lay down your weapons and return to your planet. Or we will take them from you along with your lives. There is nothing for you here but blood and death."

I thought that was pretty intimidating, but Dall and Talia seemed to think differently.

Talia's mouth dropped open when she saw it was me. Dall looked like he was going to burst. I saw a green vein pulsing above his left row of eyes.

"You would rather fight than live under our protection?" Talia was the first to recover. "You do not know what you're saying. The Voy Empire is vast and full of wonders. We are benevolent people."

"You see," I said, chuckling. "You'd fit right in with some of the politicians we have here. You use words like protection and benevolence when I think you really mean slavery and dictatorship. I've seen how you treat humans. I've seen your cages, been a private guest to your interrogation rooms. You're not fooling anyone by batting those six eyes of yours or using this little good Voy, bad Voy routine. Dall looks like he's about to erupt."

I wasn't wrong. Dall shook in a fit of rage. Each one of his four hands clenched into a tight, three-fingered fist.

"You all will feel the wrath of the Voy Empire. When I stand on your throat, you will regret these words. You are not immortal. We will take away your ability and watch you bleed like the human animal you are," Dall ground out through clenched teeth. "There will be no mercy for you. No hope. You're already dead."

"There's the Voy we all have come to know and love," I taunted, the grin I had quickly disappearing from my face. "But you should have done your home-work when choosing what species to invade. Humanity has a history paved in blood from the veins of our patriots. You see, no matter what race, creed, or nation-ality we are now, we don't like bullies. And you've somehow managed to piss off all of us. Maybe you're used to intimidating other species you come across in the galaxy, but not us, not today, not ever."

X cut the channel like an expert journalist would.

A cheer ripped from the throats around me so loud, it hurt my ears. The intensity of the moment wore off enough for me to look around at those closest to me.

Cassie was leading the war cries along with the rest of the pack that gathered around me. Yells of defiance lifted to the heavens as humanity cried in one voice.

"That was one heck of a speech," Colonel Strife said into my comms. "But let's get ready to back it up. We have incoming."

The moment of celebration was short lived as everyone hit the cement barricade and manned their weapons. The pack members and Cassie made last minute checks to their gear.

"They can kill our bodies," Preacher started, placing a closed fist in the center of our gathering.

"But they can never kill our spirit," Sam finished, placing her fist next to his.

"Can't kill our spirit," I agreed, adding my closed hand to the group followed by Echo, Angel, and Jax.

We all looked at Cassie, who stood with her hands over her chest.

"Come on," I said, jerking my head down at our fists. "You're part of this now too. It's like the howling thing."

Cassie looked unsure for one of the first times I had ever seen. She glanced to the rest of the pack for a consensus.

"Come on, we got a war to fight," Jax said.

"My arm's getting tired," Angel added.

"Can't kill our spirit," Cassie said, placing her fist in the circle.

"Let's go to work," I told them. "It's time to do what we do best."

# FOURTEEN

THERE WERE two massive turrets that shot super-heated plasma rounds. Each turret was planted on one of the dunes overlooking the attacking Voy. The operator sat in a chair that swiveled along with the turret. Series of smaller caliber weapons, rockets and launchers lined the cement wall.

I dispersed the members of the pack along our section of the dune. I stayed on top so I could see the battle unfold with Cassie to my left and Preacher to my right to call out orders and adjust as needed.

In addition to my MK II and the knife and axe recallers, I picked up a Juggernaut 270. The monstrosity of a weapon was used for firing a steady stream of rockets into the enemy. Each rocket was about the size of my forearm and fed in a short rotating clip that held eight rounds.

The Juggernaut 270 was a beast to carry, but I'd only need to lift it when firing. At the moment, it rested on the chest-high cement barrier in front of me.

"I'm superimposing an augmented reality line on the desert ground to tell you when the Voy will be in firing range," X instructed. A second later, a green line no more than a kilometer out laced the sandy ground.

"Good idea," I said, studying the movement of the massive flying bugs holding the Voy army. Above the bugs, a fleet of the Voy ships acted as escorts. The small circular fighter crafts zipped through the air. I had to wonder how a Voy could even fit in the small ship.

"The Voy are going to be within firing range in minutes," Colonel Strife said. "Julian and I are going to begin our runs. We'll do what we can to keep the enemy ships and some of these bugs out of your hair. The rest will be up to you."

"Understood," Commander Shaw answered.

"Got it," I replied.

The still sky was shredded the next moment as the GG and the Order began coordinating their runs on the enemy. Black Order ships with the red cross as their emblem strafed the Voy, firing missiles and rockets into the enemy.

The GG followed, creating a one-two punch with their own fighters entering the fray and unloading on the alien bugs.

It was both mesmerizing and sickening to witness. The Voy sent their crafts along with a half dozen of their bugs against the incoming strafing runs. The flying monolithic insects released their hold on the Voy soldiers they transported and joined the fight in the air.

The massive creatures moved in slow motion compared to the maneuverable ships in the air, but what they lacked in speed, they gained in armor.

I witnessed a dark blue Galactic Government fighter hose the left side of one of the huge bugs without leaving so much as a few smoking holes where the rounds struck the creature.

"You ready?" Commander Shaw asked, drawing my attention from the fight overhead to the ground units below. "Heavy turrets on the bugs and I'll order the Phoenix mechs to do the same. The Voy soldiers will have to be dealt with, with our smaller caliber weapons."

"Here we go!" I shouted over the sounds of destruction in the air.

The first Voy bug crossed the green line X placed for me.

"Fire!" I screamed as loud as my lungs could project.

I'd been in fights before. But I had never been in an actual all-out war. There was so much for my senses to take in. If I tried to comprehend everything that was going on at that moment, I was sure I'd be in a mental coma.

Instead, I focused on what I had to do next, then what I had to do after that, and so on and so on.

So many weapons were being fired at once and in such a close proximity, it was next to impossible to pick out individual sounds. A staccato I felt in my chest drummed a nonstop beat of rounds being dispersed into the enemy.

Both massive turrets on the dunes tore into the bug aliens along with the mechs on the flanks and the thousands of soldiers at the barricade.

Everything from mortars, to rockets, grenade launchers, tungsten rounds, plasma and laser rounds found the enemy.

The bugs hovering just over the surface of the sand tilted their head down to protect the platforms of Voy soldiers they carried. On the top of the bugs' heads, they were well-armored, absorbing everything from the turret fire to the rounds the mech units poured into them.

A wall of the colossal bugs approached hunched over their cargo to shield them from our rain of death.

One bug's head erupted in a shower of bright green gore as the turret on my side of the dune finally punctured the thick plated armor.

Another one went down on Commander Shaw's side a moment later. A cheer went up, at least I think it was a cheer. I lifted my Juggernaut and fired at the bugs, spewing a volley of rockets at the head and shoulders of the creature with little effect.

"The wings!" X shouted in my ear. "Aim for the wings. The heads are too well protected."

I changed my aim to the insect-like wings that flapped so fast, they were a constant blur. I swapped out a heavy cylinder of rockets for a new pack at my feet and went to town.

But it was too little too late. The bugs were closing in fast. I felt the weapon slam against my right shoulder over and over again as I unloaded the new charge pack on the approaching Voy monstrosity.

There was nothing wrong with my aim, but this son of a gun wasn't going down easy. Over and over again, I saw my rockets aim true and detonate on the creature's right wing that allowed it to hover over the Martian terrain.

Shouts were coming through my channel and all around me. Added to the cacophony of death the weapon fire promised, it was true hell. Screams of pain as well as victory cascaded through my ears.

Finally, my charge pack clicked dry again, but not before some visual damage was finally done to the insect creature in front of me. The monster lifted its head screeching in pain as its right wing stopped flapping altogether. A bloody green mass of gore ended at a thick stump going into its side.

The Voy soldiers underneath the beast were crushed by the massive bug's exoskeleton as it slammed into the sandy ground, pulverizing its cargo.

A roar went up from the defenders.

"Target the wings, target the wings!" I yelled into my comms. "X?"

"Sending a message to them now with the instructions," X answered.

I allowed the charge pack at the bottom of the Juggernaut to drop free at my feet. Next, I reached down to slam a fresh pack in place.

All across the line the defenders were aiming for the wings of the bugs now as opposed to their heads or backs. The enemy was closer than ever before, only a few hundred meters away.

The bugs were smarter than they looked. Now that they understood we knew how to cause them real pain, they dropped the Voy soldiers they were holding on the ground and landed beside them. Their wings folded onto their backs under a thick shell.

Now we had two problems. Thousands of screaming Voy rushed our position shooting wildly at our lines, and monstrous tank-like bugs trotted toward us at a slow but steady pace.

"Mechs and turrets on the bugs!" Commander Shaw screamed over the comms. "Everyone else take out the Voy soldiers!"

Seeing the sheer number of enemy cascading toward

us over the red Martian sand was enough to rattle even the most hardened warrior.

*We're not outnumbered,* I told myself. *This is just a target-rich environment. They're making it easy on us. Wherever we fire, we hit one of them.*

Sweat poured down my face and back. My palms were heavy with perspiration.

Hope was fading fast. There were too many and even more coming behind the first wave of soldiers carried by the bugs.

"Hey, is it wrong if I kind of hope they surround us so that we can shoot in any direction and hit an alien?" Jax asked over the comms.

"I mean, that makes sense to me," Angel growled back.

"On the brink of annihilation and you're cracking jokes?" Sam asked, feigning indignation. "Shame on you."

"That's what we do," Echo responded. "When the hour is darkest, we crack a joke and we fight. We find a way."

"We'll find a way," Preacher grunted, trying to hide the pain in his voice and failing miserably. "We'll find a way."

"Hold the line!" I screamed into my comms.

From my position on the top of the right dune, I could see what was coming for us better than most. The

Voy army was truly massive in size past the thousands of warriors racing toward our location. Past the alien bugs, I saw vehicles coming, no doubt acting as their heavy fire power as well as bringing even more aliens to attack.

None of that mattered at the moment. Right now, we were on the verge of being overrun. The Voy soldiers sprinted across the desert, firing into our lines only as a secondary act.

Their main goal was easy to see. They were warriors of hand-to-hand combat first and foremost. They wanted to bring their bladed weapons down on us, and to do so, they needed to reach us first.

New charge pack in the Juggernaut, I aimed down the dune at them and ripped open with the newly recharged weapon. I stroked the trigger just as soon as I had a target in my sights, which was not an issue.

The rockets thunked from my weapon, sending a shockwave of force into my shoulder. Over and over again, I directed the rockets at the enemy, sending showers of sand and bodies into the air wherever the rounds exploded.

Pieces of Voy body were ripped from their owners as small craters in the sand were exposed. Smoke drifted across the battleground from a thousand detonations, and still they came.

I was empty again and had to slam in my last charge pack. I should have brought more.

I alone had to be responsible for dozens of Voy deaths and still they came.

The turrets and mechs were eating away at the large bugs, but again, much too slowly. The exoskeleton on the bugs was tough enough to withstand our weapons fire in the same spot for minutes at a time.

The bugs plodded on, falling much less often than I liked.

"They're knocking at our door!" Cassie warned, sending a volley of energy rounds from her forearms into the Voy closest to her. "We've got to do something."

She wasn't wrong. The Voy were already climbing up the dune's slope. In the middle of the two dunes, they had already reached the cement barrier.

"We've got something weird going on between the dunes," Jax shouted.

"Weird? This is all weird," Angel answered. "Be more specific."

"Like Madam Eternal is going Project Nemesis on us weird," Jax replied. "Look!"

From my vantage point, I had to stand upright and look to my left on my tiptoes to get an idea of what was going on. Madam Eternal was in the process of committing suicide.

I watched with my mouth open as the woman jumped up onto the concrete barrier in front of her into the middle of the alien barrage.

# FIFTEEN

EXCEPT THAT MADAM ETERNAL wasn't committing suicide at all. The woman in the red robe looked like some kind of ancient prophetess in the light of the Martian sun. Standing like some long dead ancient queen, royal and regal as ever, the woman who told me her true name was Carly Cefrin, glowed.

With my enhanced vision, I zoomed in to see the impossible. Her eyes were shining white orbs and something like light illuminated her from the inside out. Her robes ruffled around her as if a wind had caught them. But to my knowledge, there was no wind. At least no wind of natural origin.

All around, soldiers were rallying. At first taken aback by the awesome sight, they now cheered for Madam Eternal, looking to her as a beacon of hope. In times like these, as fear sought to steal our fighting spirit, anything could be looked on as an anchor of resolve.

The Voy's reaction was not lost on the woman either. Instead of standing by shocked, they charged her, turning their weapons on Madam Eternal. The frontlines of the Voy were close enough now to unsheathe their bladed swords and knives and make a run at her.

Plasma bolts struck the space in front of Madam Eternal then dissipated just as I had seen them do with Nemesis. Rounds came at her by the hundred, crashing against whatever barrier kept her safe.

The act didn't even seem to faze her. She was doing something with her hands, moving them in very specific patterns in front of her as if she were creating or building something none of us could see.

The next moment, she extended her arms in front of her, fingers out. White tendrils shot forward from each finger like lances skewering ten of the Voy through their chests.

I hadn't really been paying attention when they went over Voy anatomy, so I wasn't sure if she was skewering them through the heart. However, the hole each white tendril left in their torso was enough to kill them.

Madam Eternal shot out these tendrils again and again. Closing her hands to recharge, they would disappear then reappear when she opened them. Each tendril snaked out in jagged lines as if it had a mind of its own, intent on finding a target.

In the space of a few heartbeats, she had taken down thirty Voy around her. Over and over again, she closed her hands then reopened them, sending out the white-hot vines of death.

Madam Eternal had saved us this first time. I had a feeling it wouldn't be the last time someone needed to step up.

"X, every available channel and exterior speakers on full?" I asked.

"Done," X answered.

"Come on!" I yelled to everyone who would listen. "Pour it on them! Give them everything you got! Keep fighting! Keep fighting!"

All around the line, soldiers from both the Galactic Government and the Coalition of Corporations unloaded. I didn't think anyone was slacking off before, but now weapons fired at a truly dizzying rate.

Those with traditional old school weapons had a pile of spent casings at their feet. Others with charge packs were beginning their own collection of empty smoking cases after being dispersed into the enemy.

It looked like we had a chance. Maybe we could hold them with Madam Eternal doing whatever kind of strange magic she was in the frontline, if magic was even the right word for it.

We might have stood a chance even with the Voy

charging over their own dead to get to us. We had enough fire power and enough weapons to keep them at bay.

The massive tank bugs were still far enough away from our frontlines that they didn't create an immediate threat. The turrets and mechs were doing their best at halting their progress.

I heard the warning a split second too late.

"Incoming!"

The cement barrier in front of me exploded outward in a million pieces. Lifted off my feet, I didn't even feel pain to begin with. I was hurled backward down the dune.

When I hit the sand on my back, I couldn't breathe. The wind had been more than knocked out of me. My body was fighting off the shock. A cold sensation touched the base of my spine. I looked up into the darkening sky, realizing for the first time that my helmet was ripped in two.

I could hear X calling for me, but I couldn't make out her words. My brain fought off the black coils of unconsciousness. All around the frontline, explosions were going off. Fires spread along the walls.

My mind raced with images from my past. I saw myself getting beat up in an alley. I remembered training in an underground facility with the rest of the pack. I saw myself going on missions with them as we doled out the justice that Immortal Corp decided.

Then I saw Amber. I saw Cryx and the Way settlers. I saw the prisoners the Voy captured and placed in prison. I saw Dall.

I WASN'T A DOCTOR. I didn't know how concussions worked or what was done to my brain during the process of turning me into whatever it was I was, but the trauma to my head triggered another buried memory.

I was in an underground bunker. At least I think it was underground. Everything was dark grey and black from the floor to the walls and ceiling. A soft squishy mat sprang up under my bare feet.

All the other members in the Pack Protocol were present from Echo to Sam and even Amber. We stood in a line dressed in black pants and tank tops of the same color.

"Here, here, here," Preacher said, walking in front of our line, pointing to a different part of his body as he said the words. First he motioned to his eyes, his throat, then his crotch. "All soft parts of the body that should be your target if you find yourself in a bind. Nothing's off limits. There's no honor in dying. If your back is against the wall, then you do whatever you have to do to come out of it alive. Make every strike count and disable your opponent as quickly as possible. More than likely, we'll be up against multiple targets at once."

I nodded with the others, looking down at my arms and legs. It was one of those dreams where it was really me seeing through my own eyes. I looked around for X. She usually made it into these memories since it was played in the theatre of my mind. For some reason, she wasn't in this one, at least not yet.

"Daniel, would you assist me in a demonstration?" Preacher asked, motioning me forward.

"Watch your balls," Jax whispered to my right. He kept his eyes on Preacher and refused to crack a grin as if he hadn't said it at all.

I walked forward to join Preacher in front of the rest of the pack. He took up a fighting stance across from me. I did the same, bending my legs at the knees, both hands up, palms open.

My breathing was even and calm.

Without warning, Preacher came at me with a series of blows he used to get in close. I batted them to the side with my open hands giving ground. Preacher's onslaught of strikes was only intended to close distance. Once he was inside my guard, he brought a knee up.

I slammed both my hands down, forced to take a strike to the side of my neck from a sideways chop of his left hand. The nerves in my neck nearly sent my body into shutdown mode.

I stumbled. That was a bad sign for anyone facing a member of our group. Preacher took my legs out and landed on top of me. He pressed both thumbs into my eyes then released his hold.

"Nothing's off limits," Preacher said, rising to his feet and offering me a hand, aiding me to my own. "We fight to survive. We fight to win no matter the cost."

I accepted his hand.

He pulled me to my feet.

"Let's partner up and practice," Preacher said.

Angel joined me with a wry grin on her face. "I thought for sure he was going to make it so you couldn't have kids. Then I thought he was going to give you an eye patch and you two were going to be twins."

"Not sure the whole eye patch look is my thing," I said, taking up my stance. "He can pull it off, but I'm more of a two-eyed kind of guy."

The next series of scenes were of getting thrown around and doing my fair share of throwing as well. It was strange to practice such a brutal art on friends that I would have considered family.

These were all people that I genuinely liked and cared for and here we were trading punches and practicing the art of war.

"Don't hold back," Preacher called out as we traded partners. "You're doing no one any favors if you don't practice with your full potential. You're only cheating yourself and your partner."

It was just my luck that my next partner was Jax. The largest member of the Pack Protocol had yet to grow a beard, but he still wore his signature Mohawk.

"Sorry, Danny," Jax said, cracking his neck. "I can't take it easy on you this round. Teacher says so."

"When have you ever taken it easy on me?" I asked the big man.

"Good point," Jax said with a wide grin. "Ready?"

"Hold," Preacher called out as the doors to our room slid open from the middle. A series of lab-coated technicians walked through the door.

A woman with chocolate brown hair and large framed glasses came to me with a steel briefcase. Her nametag read Doctor Patmos.

"Sorry to interrupt your session," Doctor Patmos called out to the room. "We just need a quick sample and we'll be gone."

While Doctor Patmos opened her case and removed a syringe, I noticed there was a technician for each member of the pack. From what I could tell, it was standard process for this to happen. No one lifted a finger as if it were out of the ordinary.

In my memory, I could see what she was doing, but I either couldn't or didn't have the desire to stop her.

For her part, Doctor Patmos seemed pretty normal. I wasn't sure what I was expecting, some kind of mad scientist behind the creation of the Pack or something else. She gave me a smile and held my left arm in her own for a moment finding the vein in the crook of my elbow.

"How've you been feeling, Daniel?" Doctor Patmos asked with a genuine look in her eye. "You've been training hard."

"Great," I answered as she slid the needle in my arm and began to draw the crimson blood.

"You know you're the first to show changes. Your very DNA is evolving, thanks to the program. Samantha and her own unique transformation are following close behind. The difference is that you've accepted your change while she fights hers," Doctor Patmos explained. "If there was a way you could talk to her. Tell her it's okay to let go. That her change is unique and special. I think that might go a long way."

"Uh huh," I said, hearing everything the doctor was explaining to me. My attention, however, was diverted to the open briefcase at our feet. Inside the briefcase was a piece of foam cut out to hold the syringe and three tubes. One of the tubes yet to be filled was labeled with the name "Nemesis."

# SIXTEEN

"DANIEL, DANIEL, CAN YOU HEAR ME?" X was asking in a panicked voice. "Daniel, are you there?"

"What—what happened?" I asked, trying to sit up. Then the pain came, collapsing my chest and tearing into my lungs.

I winced and lay back down. Each breath was a new lesson in agony. I remembered my suppressed memory, every detail, every word that was said, but this was neither the place nor time to go on some kind of self-realizing journey.

"Voy artillery happened," Cassie said, skidding to a stop by my side. "You need to be taken back?"

"No, no, I'm good," I lied. "I just need a minute. Help me up."

Cassie pulled me to my feet. My head swam both

with the pain and a new wave of fatigue that hit me from the head down.

"Daniel," Cassie said with an arm over my shoulder. "You don't look good."

"That's just my normal face," I told her, spitting blood. "Get me back in the fight. I'll heal. I'll be fine!"

I had to shout the last few words as a new wave of enemy artillery battered our line of defenders.

"That artillery is going to eat us alive," Madam Eternal said over the comms. "There's a limit to even my powers."

"Yeah, your powers we'll have to talk about later," Commander Shaw answered. "But I agree. Colonel Strife, Julian, are you able to get to those Voy artillery units?"

"Negative." Colonel Strife's voice sounded stressed. "They have their own crafts swarming above their heavy artillery. Which is good for you at the moment, since it keeps them busy, but bad for us getting to them."

"A ground assault is the only way." Julian's voice cracked over the channel. "I've already sent in a squad to try and take out the artillery and they didn't come back. The Voy have all their air support defending it against us now."

"What's the fastest way to get there?" I asked, still struggling up the side of the dune. My heart dropped in my chest when I saw the smoking remains of the turret at the crest of the dune. One of our greatest assets had fallen victim to the Voy artillery.

What remained of the turret was a smoking mass of charred wreckage. The Valkyrie operator behind the turret was gone.

"We'll have to try and punch a hole through their lines," Wesley said, sounding none-too-enthusiastic about the possibility.

We finally reached the top of the dune and looked out over the carnage that was on the battlefield. The morning was gone. It was midday and the sun was high and hot overhead.

Commander Shaw's Phoenix mech had moved from their positions guarding our flanks and engaged the massive bug creatures on the frontline. We would have been able to stand toe to toe with the Voy despite their superior numbers if it hadn't been for their artillery pounding our lines.

The Voy gave no pause when it came to possibly firing on their own units. Voy soldiers still ran at our defenses as if there were some kind of reward to be won for the first to break through our lines.

More than once, I saw a Voy actually reach the cement barricade, only to be eviscerated by one of their own heavy artillery rounds.

"We're taking substantial losses on the barricade," Commander Shaw yelled. "They're making a push for—"

The channel went dead.

"Shaw, Shaw, can you hear me?" I asked.

"Shaw, report in," Wesley barked.

Nothing.

"We move back away from the barricade and let them have it," Madam Eternal suggested. "The losses are too heavy here. If we pull back, we'll be out of range of their artillery at least for the time being until we can figure something out."

"There's no cover behind you," Colonel Strife warned. "You'll be fighting amongst the ammunition and supply tents."

"Let's do it," I said as another round took out an entire section of the cement bunker beside me and the soldiers hunched behind it for cover.

"Pull back and we'll come up with a plan," Julian agreed. "It's our only play at the moment."

"I opened the channel to all lines," X informed me, already anticipating what we needed to do next. "You're on."

"Pull back!" I yelled into the channel. "We're getting out of range of the Voy artillery. Pull back to the ammunition tents and set up what defenses you can. Pack. Let's buy them some time. Rally with Madam Eternal."

A series of "rogers" and "understoods" came back.

My healing factor was already making walking and breathing easier.

Cassie and I headed down the ridge firing to our right into the enemy climbing up the dune. As much as I knew I needed to focus, the battles taking place beyond our lines between the mech warriors and the bugs was astounding. What advantage the bugs had on the mechs for size and armor, the mechs had durability and speed.

They clashed over and over again. Both the Voy artillery and soldiers willing to leave our giant armor units alone and concentrate on overrunning our lines.

We made our way down the slope to the valley in between the two dunes.

Our units were already pulling back to set up near the ammunition and supply depots. Madam Eternal stood with her shining white eyes and sharp tendrils still coming out of her hands.

As I got closer, I could tell how worn she was. I had no way to measure the amount of effort or energy it took her to do whatever she was doing, but I understood by the sweat on her face and the way her brow knitted, she didn't have much left.

"The book," Madam Eternal said without looking at me. "The Relic, Daniel. It doesn't matter what anyone wants anymore. It matters what we must do to survive."

"I know," I said, running so many scenarios through my mind at once, they flashed past me like a speeding dropship.

*What if the Relic doesn't work? What if it does work and it backfires? What does the book do?* These questions and more demanded answers for which I had none.

"We're pulling back. The Pack is covering the retreat. Come on," I added on an afterthought. "You get that Relic ready but don't do anything until I tell you."

Madam Eternal jumped back down from the concrete barrier. The white light vanished from her eyes and hands. She gave me a quick nod, taking in my appearance for the first time.

Half my helmet was missing along with a fair amount of blood dripping down my face I had not taken the time to clean. My armor was shredded in a dozen different locations.

"You don't look so good," Madam Eternal said in a worried voice. "I could—"

"I feel as good as new," I told her, waving her off. "Go, they'll be here soon."

Madam Eternal nodded. She retreated to the rear supply tents that now acted as our last line of defense.

I looked around at what had been the frontlines a few moments before. There were bodies, weapons and ammunition canisters, broken pieces of the cement barricade, and smoking holes where the Voy artillery impacted everywhere.

There was a brief lull in the battle as the Voy gathered themselves for the next push.

Cassie and the rest of the Pack rallied around me.

Time was short. We had seconds before the Voy would overrun our barriers and swarm once more.

I remembered the look into the past the concussion afforded me. I remembered the vial being labeled Nemesis and more importantly what Doctor Patmos had said about Sam. How she knew how the treatment we went through made her different but fought it instead of accepting it. I wondered if Echo was the same way.

"We're going to form a line and hold them here to buy the others enough time to set up shop." I threw a hand to where what remained of our forces set up whatever barricades and weapons they could about fifty meters from our location. "Make sure you have your comm lines open. We'll need to fall back soon. They'll overrun us if we don't."

"Is this a suicide mission?" Jax asked, already shrugging off his armor so it wouldn't inhibit his change. "I mean, I'm cool with it if it is, but I just want to know what I'm getting myself into here."

"I guess that's up to you and how well you can fight," Preacher said, pulling the handle of his cane from the sheath hiding what it truly was. A blade as long as a sword extended out. It hummed with a dull red.

"I thought you lost that when the Voy took you?" Angle asked.

"Nothing's ever really lost," Preacher said with a knowing smile. "The blade and I share a bond."

"I'm not going to try and figure out that one right now," Sam said, already moving to take her place on our line. "Come on; the Voy know what we're up to."

I was about to ask how she could know that when she touched a finger from the side of her helmet where her ear was to the sky above.

Sam was right. The constant battering of explosions around the barricade was gone. The Voy suspended their barrage for the time being, realizing we had pulled back.

Sweat covered me from head to toe. Hunger was present, but only as an afterthought. We stood in the valley between the two dunes. This was where the Voy would attack; it was the easiest point of entry. The same point Madam Eternal had been defending during the battle.

They would stream in here first, then when we held them, they would climb the dunes and come in to flank us. That was when we had to fall back.

"Sam, Echo," I said, going over to my left where the pair took up their positions. "I don't know if this makes sense to you, but if you have any kind of idea what ability you have, this would be the time to use it. Don't fight it. Embrace whatever it is. We can use all the help we can get."

Echo nodded.

Sam was silent at first. "What if it's something we can't control. Like Jax?"

I remembered the hulking figure Jax turned into when he activated what made his own DNA different. He was a raging brute just as likely to hurt one of us as the enemy. His most primal being given permission to take over and rage.

"I know you'll be able to keep It under control," I told her. "It's part of you. You'll be able to harness it. I have faith."

At this point, I knew I had been spending way too much time with Brother Enoch and the Way settlers. I couldn't believe I just used the word "faith" right now. But willingly facing down a horde of four-armed alien invaders and believing we could win, what other term was there?

I took my place dead center in the middle of the valley between the two dunes. Jax, Angel, and Preacher to my right. Cassie, Sam, and Echo to my left.

"I'll come find you," Angel said to Jax in a hushed tone. "If you can't rein in that beast inside of you, just run. When this is all over, I'll come find you."

"Thank you," Jax said, removing the last bit of armor from his body. He had even taken off his synth suit underneath. He stood in black skintight shorts he'd shred as soon as he made the change.

The Voy lifted their voices, screaming in front of us as they came.

I wasn't one to go silent.

"I've spent a long time trying to figure out who I am," I roared to the dead space in front of me. "What I've found out is that I'm someone who's going to die empty. I'm going to give you everything I have. My dying breath, my last swing, everything! Let's break their will to fight! Are you with me!?"

Six other voices lifted to the heavens in roars.

The Voy came.

# SEVENTEEN

THE VOY RUSHED EN masse just like we suspected. I had my MK II set to fire explosive rounds into the enemy. Like before, they fired their weapons only as an afterthought to crossing the distance and getting their hands on us with their blades.

Black laser rounds scorched the ground around us. From the peripheral vision on my right, I saw Jax make his change.

I had only witnessed it once before. The way the Pack protocol testing had changed Jax's DNA was by giving him the ability to tap into his most primal form. Ripped corded muscles bulked over his already impressive physique as he grew two sizes. His eyes went red, fangs sprouted from his mouth.

The change only took seconds and then he was off. As naked as the day he was born and a hundred times as deadly. Weapons fire from the Voy bounced off his skin as if it were made of the same shielding Madam Eternal and the man named Nemesis used.

I wished I could have seen him at work, but I had enough to deal with. A laser round struck my left shin, sending a stab of pain up my body and taking me down to a knee.

I grunted, ripping off the half helmet that only covered a portion of my face and went to work. It was easy finding targets when they willingly rushed you at a twenty-meter distance. I made them pay, that was for sure.

My MK II smoked as I squeezed the trigger time and time again. The explosive rounds detonated on impact, taking two, three, even four Voy at a time. Still, it wasn't enough in the face of their numbers.

"Enemy artillery is making a push forward," Julian said in our comms. Although my helmet was gone I still had access to the channels thanks to X. "We'll do what we can, but we can't stop them. We're outnumbered in the air three to one and now they're turning their artillery skyward."

"The weapons are not only capable of firing on ground units but air units as well," Colonel Strife confirmed. "We'll do what we can."

I heard all of this as I stroked my trigger time and time again.

Cassie was on my left. Her right forearm doled out

blaster rounds while her left sprouted a large shield from it like a fan and covered her body. She came over to me, placing her shield in front of us both as we fired into the enemy.

I was out of explosive rounds faster than I thought possible and switched to gas.

Jax, unable to keep his animal rage in check, howled at the moon and rushed the enemy. I saw him take Voy in his hands and rip the aliens in half.

Angel was there one second then blinked out of sight the next, enacting her own ability to go invisible.

Preacher protected our right flank with his red sword swirling in motion. Even without his enhanced capabilities, he was still a force to be reckoned with.

"Angel!" I shouted. "Preacher, he—"

"I got his back," Angel said from somewhere to my right.

"Daniel, to your left," X said in my head. "Sam."

Voy rounds pinged off Cassie's shield. I looked over to my left in time to see Sam extend a hand. I didn't see anything come from her hand, but the half dozen Voy in front of her were thrown backward as if they had been hit by a dropship.

Again and again, Sam threw her hands out as if she were controlling forces only she could see. Where she wiped her hands across the battlefield Voy were crushed or thrown into the air.

Echo fought beside her, still using his shotgun like a heavy blaster. If he had figured out what his ability was, I didn't see it.

More Voy rounds battered against Cassie's shield.

I was out of gas rounds and went to the good old traditional tungsten steel rods. I would be out of those as well soon and down to knockout rounds that didn't seem right for the occasion.

"Hey, thanks for the assist," I said to Cassie as I ducked behind her shield for a quick second of relief. We were huddled so close, I rubbed against her side. In any other circumstance, cuddling this close might seem awkward, but right now, awkwardness was the last thing on my mind.

"Daniel." Cassie ignored how close we were. "We've got trouble."

"Tell me about it," I said.

"No," Cassie shouted back. "I mean, something's happening."

I popped up over her shield, sending off another round of bolts into the enemy. I took one in the forehead and another in one of his six eyes.

Cassie was right. Instead of the Voy racing toward us, their ranks were parting to let someone or something through the middle. Whatever the Voy were making room for wasn't good.

At least four Voy wearing black masks and holding

what looked like rocket launchers came to the front-lines. A whomping sound of gas canisters being launched filled the air as a volley arched toward us.

"The gas," Preacher yelled, exhausted. "The Voy neutralized my healing ability. They're going to do the same to you now with the gas!"

There was no time to act. The gas canisters were already in the air. I didn't have my helmet. Neither did Jax. There was a chance Echo, Angel, and Sam would be safe with their helmets still intact, but who knew what kind of gas the Voy had concocted. What if it wasn't filtered out by their helmets?

For the first time in that fight, real terror gripped me. If we lost our abilities, this fight was over.

The canisters spun toward us end over end, spewing out white gas.

They were a few meters from dropping on us when they stopped in midair. Four canisters ceased to spin and instead stood upright in place, the gas harmlessly wafting skyward and even back toward the Voy in the slight breeze of the Martian landscape.

I looked around confused.

Apparently, I wasn't the only one. The four Voy in black masks carrying the gas canisters' launchers looked at one another in wonder. One of the idiots even tried hitting his launcher and shaking it as if that was going to help.

I searched the area around me for an answer.

Sam stood with both her hands out skyward. She clenched her fists then threw the canister back in a sideways motion. The canisters struck the sand near the Voy harmlessly and then burrowed into the dirt as if they were small animals with minds of their own to get down deep into the planet's crust.

Sam didn't stop there. The four Voy carrying the canister were about to fire again. The woman from the Badlands clenched her hands, crumpling their weapons, then lifted the four Voy into the air as one.

They screamed and clawed against the invisible force lifting them higher and higher into the air. Sam must have taken them up a good twenty to thirty stories before she let them fall.

They came down screaming to the sandy ground that now acted like a wall of steel. Their bodies broke and the screaming stopped.

The rallying Voy were caught in a moment of debate. Their plan to neutralize us gone, the Voy stood staring. They still outnumbered us by more than I'd like to guess, but in that moment, time slowed.

I was out of anything in my MK II drum besides nonlethal knockout rounds. In retrospect, I should have swapped those out for more explosive or even regular rounds.

Live and learn, I guess.

I holstered my MK II and stood up, unsheathing the

knife and axe at my belt. The recallers I wore on each wrist hummed to life.

Fighting from ships somewhere in the distance could still be heard as well as the mechs that remained as they battled the bugs.

"The mechs are taking heavy losses." Wesley's voice broke the silence. "I've ordered them to retreat. Daniel, I'm sorry. You're about to have a bug problem very soon."

That made my mind up for me. A tiny insane voice spoke into my ear to charge the overwhelming numbers of Voy. A crazy idea that we could break them here and now as they witnessed their best plan to neutralize us die in the sand.

With the bugs coming and the artillery still able to fire on us, it was too risky.

"Retreat!" I yelled across the sand instead. "Sam and I will provide cover. The rest of you retreat back to the line."

I saw Angel blink back into focus. She helped Preacher back, supporting him with his arm draped over her shoulders. She glanced to me and shouted, "Jax!?"

The madman was gone. Too far into the Voy ranks to be seen.

"We'll get him," I promised her. "We'll find him. He'll be okay."

That was the hardest thing I had yet to do. I knew

Jax could take care of himself. I knew I couldn't talk him down even if I did find him. I had to trust that just like before, he would be fine and we'd find him when this was all done.

Echo ran forward to help Angel carry Preacher back.

Cassie ignored my instructions. She joined Sam and me as we covered the others' retreat.

Sam was a wrecking ball with her hands dancing out from side to side as she picked up Voy and flung them into the air. She slammed a few down, crushing them with her invisible force. Others she sent hurtling into their own ranks behind them.

She made the moves quickly. She was focused, but just like Madam Eternal, I knew she couldn't go on forever. It was a temporary fix at best. A temporary solution I was grateful for but still one that was fleeting.

The disturbing thing was the Voy didn't chase us like they had before. Instead of coming after us, they seemed content to fire on our position. They took up their own defensive position at the cement barrier that had once marked our own lines.

There were so many bodies of both Voy and our own on the ground, the scene looked like something out of a nightmare. Images of the nightmare I had the previous night cascaded through my mind.

"What are they doing?" I asked in my comms as the three of us made it back to the rest of the defenders.

The area with the ammunition tents had been set up with whatever would work as barriers. Tables were overturned, empty ammunition canisters and crates used as defensive structure with heavy repeaters on top.

"They're waiting," Wesley said in a cold hard voice. "The mechs that remain are retreating around your position. They'll join you at the rear. The Voy are waiting for their bugs and their artillery to get into place."

The defeat in Wesley's voice wasn't obvious, but to anyone who spent time with him, it was obvious he wasn't excited about our odds.

"We're pulling back," Colonel Strife added. "It was a good run, but we did all we could. We'll have to head back to the city and try to set up a last stand there, hoping we hold out until the Galactic Government arrives."

"They're still a day out," Julian answered. "We should make that stand now."

"Either way, the choice must be made quickly," Madam Eternal said, coming up to me with the Relic in her hands. "It's time."

I looked down at the book in the woman's hands. I felt exhausted, drained, but when I looked up and saw everyone looking at me, I knew I had to do something.

"That artillery is moving in," Colonel Strife answered. "We need to pull back or make a move now."

"Look!" someone shouted, pointing to the pair of dunes we had defended. The Voy bugs were back. The goliath creatures waded through the Voy ranks to act as a frontline shield for the next push. There were still dozens of them.

## EIGHTEEN

THE VOY STOPPED FIRING, letting in a single figure that wore a plain white robe and bright silver armor underneath. I couldn't see what the Voy carried to make his voice echo across the battlefield, but I sure as crip recognized who was talking.

"Humans!" Dall's voice carried over the battleground. "You are outnumbered and out-gunned and have been defeated multiple times during this battle. Will you not see the truth of this? Surrender now and bend your knee or we will attack with the full power of our army again. This time, we will not stop. We'll run through you and straight to your city to burn it to the ground."

Anger welled in my heart. I was only able to keep my temper to make a final decision. I knew Julian would argue. Madam Eternal would agree. Wesley and Colonel Strife stood somewhere in the middle.

"This is my call," I said into the comms. "I'll take full responsibility for the fall out. Madam Eternal is going to open the Relic. That's all there is to it. You heard Dall; even if we run, they'll be right behind us."

"Do it," Wesley answered.

"I agree," Colonel Strife said.

There was a long pause.

"Cassie, I hope you're right about the Relic and for all these years the Order has been wrong, for all of our sakes," Julian finally said. "May God have mercy on our souls for what we are about to do."

"How long will it take?" I asked Madam Eternal.

"Minutes, maybe longer," Madam Eternal answered, running a hand over the cover of the book.

"I'm going to need more than 'maybe' here," I said, not able to keep my temper in check any longer.

"Excuse me for not knowing exactly how long the Relic will take to be active." Madam Eternal's eyes flashed white. "I don't do this every day. The book has not been opened for centuries."

"I'll buy you some time," I said, walking out from behind our meager defenses. "Hurry."

"Daniel." Cassie caught my arm. "What are you going to do?"

"Dall likes to talk," I answered. "I'm going to go let him talk."

I sheathed both weapons as I walked toward the Voy lines. To be honest, I wasn't sure how I was still moving. My body was battered, and I hadn't drank or eaten anything in far too long.

"Don't do anything stupid," X warned me inside my head. "I mean it. You don't have to be the martyr here."

"Ahhh, come on, X," I said. "You know me."

"Yes, and that's why I'm worried," X answered.

"Hey, how come you weren't in that last flashback?" I asked, my boots crunching over the sand as I crossed into the space between the two armies. "Usually, I see you in a past memory or dream or flashback."

"I was there," X answered in a soft tone. "I—I just didn't want to interrupt you. It seemed like an important memory."

"You never interrupt me." I jerked my chin toward Dall, who now stood only a few meters in front of me. "Ugly, on the other hand, pisses me off."

"Daniel Hunt," Dall said with an amused laugh. "I hoped you had survived this far."

The Voy crossed both pairs of arms. His white cloak fell off his shoulders. He wore some kind of metal armor like the rest of his soldiers, but his was more ornate. Six eyes blinked at me awaiting a response.

I didn't want to disappoint.

"Dall, you cheeky minx," I said with a smile that didn't touch my eyes. "I was hoping I'd get to see you again."

"You should be careful what you wish for," Dall tilted his head to the side to look around me. "It seems your forces are broken, nearly half of what they once were. The crafts you have in the air are smoldering, those walking battle tanks barely able to move. Look for yourself."

In the hope to keep the jabber-jaw going as long as possible, I played along.

I looked up into the sky. He wasn't lying. Smoke came from more than a few crafts fighting to stay in the sky. Colonel Strife and Julian had been fighting just as hard as we were on the ground, coordinating attacks, refueling and resupplying their forces in the air. For every three of our crafts still airborne, I saw at least one had some kind of issue, be it smoking, limping through the air, or otherwise.

The mechs were in no better shape. A handful had made it back around to the rear of our forces. The giant units smoked and sizzled. One was missing an arm; all of them were dented and scraped.

"This is it for you," Dall said again. "At the edge of hope, I think it is due justice that it is you who will surrender."

"That little stunt you pulled trying to gas us was cute." I turned back to face Dall. "You should have had something better than that."

"And what makes you think we don't?" Dall asked with a wicked smile. "The Voy empire is vast. Our scientists are on the cutting edge of experimentation your kind can only dream of."

Dall produced a syringe from the inside of his folds.

"We have engineered an elixir that will affect the Voy just like your own has changed you, but ours is stronger and even more effective." Dall eyed the amber fluid in his syringe with manic glee. "I was hoping we'd get to test it on our Voy for this fight. Too bad we managed to crush you so easily and you decided to surrender."

I spat to the side, less because I really had too much saliva and more to buy time and seem tough.

"I didn't say anything about surrendering," I corrected him. "That was all you running your mouth. Why don't we see exactly how effective that serum is? Just you and me, right now, right here."

Dall eyed me suspiciously. As much as I hated him, he wasn't stupid. He knew I was stalling for time. The question now was if I could push his ego far enough where he wouldn't care and play along to save face.

"I thought the Voy Empire was vast and magical and full of pink clouds and all that," I egged him on. "Warriors of fame and legend and blah, blah, blah. All I see in front of me is a stunted Voy with a big mouth."

"I will not stand here and allow you to speak of the Voy Empire in such a way!" Dall shouted. I could see flecks of spit flying from his green lips. It was disgusting. "Do not think me a fool. I know exactly what you're doing, but it won't matter. You stalling for time is simply staying the hand of the inevitable for a moment longer. We're tracking your reinforcements en route. They will never reach you in time. When they arrive, we will have slaughtered you all. We will raise another force of Voy soldiers from their cocoons. Then we will deal with them if they refuse to surrender."

"I'm getting tired of talking." I yawned and stretched my arms before eyeing the syringe in his hand. "You going to pump yourself full of juice so we can get on with this or are we going to discuss the weather next?"

A vein in Dall's head pulsed as he set his jaw. If Voy could turn red with anger, this one did.

Instead of addressing me, Dall turned to his army. He conversed with them in a series of clicks and screeches I didn't understand. Whatever he said sent an uproar of shouts through the Voy army so loud, I winced.

When the shouting finally died down, I thought I might have missed my chance. For all I knew, Dall told them to all rush me at once.

"You going to share with the rest of the class?" I asked, steeling my voice and fighting down all the pent-up aggression I felt.

"I told them the human scum thinks he's goading me into a fight that I do not want," Dall said to me

with a smile. "I told them you will pay for your inso-
lence with your life. I'm going to enjoy this."

With that, Dall plunged the end of the syringe into
the side of his neck. He pressed a button on the tool
that plunged the serum into his body.

Nothing happened.

I was about to crack another joke at him as we all
waited in stunned silence when I saw his body spasm.
It was like he was going to throw up but kept it in as
another wave of motion rolled over his frame.

Dall screeched then fell to his knees and hands. His
body began to elongate and widen.

Unlike Jax's own transformation, this was something very different. The otherwise skinny Voy's arms
doubled in size with spikes coming out of his elbows.
His fingers turned to hardened claws. More spikes and
hard edges came out of his cheeks and eyebrows. His
eyes were black orbs.

He was already taller than I was, but now he was
wider as well. The clothing on his body fell off. His
armor ripped at the straps and slid off his now greyish
skin. Scales that looked like rock covered him from
head to toe.

Maybe the worst part of it all was the fact he was
completely nude, and as much as I didn't want to look,
the lack of any kind of genitalia was staring me in the
face.

"Are you sure this was a good idea?" X asked in my head.

Dall began to laugh. The voice was deeper, not his own. He looked over his body, his four arms and naked skin.

"I never said it was a good idea," I said to X, swallowing hard. "It was the only idea I had. If we live through this, I'm definitely having nightmares."

"Therapy would be a wise choice," X said. I could hear the tension in her voice despite the joke. She was worried about me.

Dall was now a good foot, maybe foot and a half taller than me. He probably outweighed me by fifty to sixty pounds as well. If his change was anything like Jax's, his skin was going to be nearly impossible to penetrate.

Dall laughed again, motioning to the weapons at my belt.

"Human versus Voy," Dall bellowed. "This is what you wanted. No weapons."

"And you're going to remove those, I assume?" I asked, directing my gaze to the four hands of razor sharp claws on his arms. "No way. I'll keep my weapons."

"I'm in contact with Madam Eternal on another channel," X informed me. "She's working on the Relic but needs more time."

"Of course she does," I said, unsheathing the axe

and knife at my belt. I held the handles tight as if they would give me some kind of strength. "Tell her time's running out."

A war cry went up from the Voy's side again. The smell of death assailed my nostrils not for the first time that day. Despite the number of dead, there were still so many of them. How were there so many of them? We had to have killed thousands.

I was heartened by the cries of my own side behind me. I could imagine Cassie, Preacher, Angel, and Sam encouraging the round of cries.

"I'm going to enjoy tearing your limbs from your body," Dall said, cracking knuckles on all four of his hands. He rolled his neck around his shoulders. "As the head of this little coalition, it will be good for your kind to watch you die."

# NINETEEN

DALL WAS nothing short of an abomination. And I meant that in the absolute worst way. He sprinted toward me with superhuman speed, or I guess in his case, super alien speed.

So many arms swiped at me, I barely avoided them as I rolled to my left. Jumping to my feet, I ducked another claw and then blocked a blow from his lower right arm. The hard stone-like substance his skin had become sparked off the blade from my hatchet.

Another series of ducks and dodges and I separated myself from him to buy me a moment to think of how I was going to do this.

*Skin might as well be armor,* I thought to myself. *I'm not going to out-muscle him. Speed is only going to save me for so long. Even you have your limits.*

Dall laughed.

"Is that your plan?" he asked. "You're going to run and dodge me until I die of old age?"

"That might be sooner than you think," I said, taking in a deep breath to calm my racing heart. "You don't look like you're aging well."

Dall smiled at me, revealing rows of sharpened teeth that had not been there before his transformation.

He lifted his head to the sky and screamed something unintelligible before charging again.

This time, he connected with a claw down my face and another across my ribs. The strike that hit my ribs was halted by my armor, but my face was fair game. I felt white-hot pain open across my face as three claws ripped lines from the corner of my right eye down to my left cheek.

I hammered my axe down at his arm with no effect besides a shower of sparks erupting from his rock-like skin. I dragged my blade across his torso with the same effect.

Dall used the time it took me to mount my failed attack to grab my arms with both his lower hands. He pinned my arms to my sides with so much force, I thought my forearms were going to snap.

Lifting me off the ground, Dall held me like a trophy for all to see.

"Look! Look! Is this your champion? Is this the

savior of your people!?" Dall mocked. "Watch as I tear him from within."

"Daniel?" X said in my head. "Daniel, you need help. Let me call the others."

"No," I grunted. "We need more time. Calling—calling them will just—start another fight we—can't win."

"What are you sputtering, human?" Dall asked, bringing me in so close to his grotesque face, I could smell something like stale meat on his breath. "Are you pleading for your life now? Speak louder that all might hear."

My arms were pinned to my side, making my weapons even more useless against Dall than they already were. Feet dangling from the ground, I stared into his six black eyes.

"I said—I said your breath smells horrible. You need to switch up your diet or start flossing or something. Really, it's embarrassing," I managed to push the words past my lips despite the pain in my arms.

Dall gave me a wicked grin.

What came next was pain in the most primal form. I heard it before I felt it. Dall twisted my left arm backward. The sound was like a dry leaf or brush of some kind being stepped on. Then pain exploded so violently in my shoulder and head, I thought I might pass out for the umpteenth time.

"Raaawww!" I screamed into the night as Dall dropped me to the ground.

"Daniel, Daniel, let me call them," X pleaded. "I'm connecting the others now. You have to let them come!"

"I'm not going to watch you die!" Cassie shouted over the comms. "We're coming!"

"No!" I screamed past the pain. "No, I can do this. Let me do this!"

Somewhere behind me, Dall was speaking in Voy to his own soldiers, no doubt taunting me or puffing out his chest. He ignored me for the time being.

"How much more—more time before the Relic is ready?" I gasped, trying and failing to hide the agony in my shoulder.

"Four minutes," Madam Eternal said. "No more."

"Give us the word," Preacher said. "Give us the word and we'll come. We all will. Even your healing ability has its limits."

"No, no, I'm good," I lied, cradling my left arm close to my body. I fought my way to my knees. I faced our own lines. I could see Cassie and the others looking at me as if they were willing me to get back to my feet. "I can do this. Four minutes. I can do anything for four minutes."

"You haven't replenished your body with food or the water it needs to fuel your accelerated healing," Sam warned. "You'll still heal but not as fast."

"I've got this," I said, fighting to my feet and turning around to Dall, who was still going on in his native tongue to the Voy army.

"Hey! Ugly!" I wobbled on my feet. "Still don't speak Voy. In English so we can all laugh at you together."

Dall didn't say anything this time. Instead, he stalked over to me and taught me what true pain really was. My left arm hung useless. With my right, I managed to block a few blows, but at this point, it was all defense and a losing defense at that.

A series of strikes to my body later and I was sure my ribs were cracked despite my armor. I bled from my lip and my right eye was swelling. Somewhere in the manic assault, I lost my axe.

I still managed to hold on to the knife in my right hand as I fell to my knees. I felt sick to my stomach, weak and exhausted all at once. My own blood painted the sand in front of me.

Dall raged once more, screeching to the night air as he laid into me. The furious blows he landed on me came less and less often as the minutes ticked by. Even he had to breathe. He was wearing down whether he wanted to admit it or not.

My use as his personal punching bag tapped his endurance. Moving all of those limbs and bulky muscles meant energy expended. Dall towered over me, taking in long gasps of breath. His chest heaved.

I sat on my knees in front of him, so much blood coming from my body and soaking the sand in front of me, I wondered how I could lose so much of the necessary fluid and still be conscious.

Images of the flashback I had earlier that day ran through my mind. Preacher's training session, the doctor coming in, the Nemesis name on the syringe. An idea from that memory hit me like a lightning bolt.

"Daniel, enough," X pleaded. "Let me call for help."

"Daniel, Daniel, we're coming," Cassie said over my channel.

"No," I managed with a cough. My mouth was dry of saliva but full of my own blood. "I've spent—a long time trying to figure out who I am. More time not liking who I was. But I've discovered one thing about myself."

Dall looked at me with pure malice in his eyes. Still trying to catch his breath, he shook his head. "What are you sputtering about?"

I ignored him.

"For all my faults, for all my sins of the past, I've found out one thing about who I am," I said, looking up at Dall through my swollen eyes. "I'm the guy who—gets—back—up!"

With everything I had, with all that I was, I sprang to my feet. I lunged at Dall with my one good arm. The knife, still in my right hand, slipped through his lower left eye like a hot poker through a thin ball of pus.

It was disgusting and that was saying a lot from me. I'd seen some pretty messed-up stuff. If I had energy for being sick, I might have vomited.

The black eyeball popped like a pimple as bloody ooze fell down his face, my knife, and hand.

Dall lifted each of his four hands to his face, screaming in pain.

He fell backward, batting violently at me and the knife.

I let my grip of the weapon go, falling back to the ground on unsteady feet. That was it. That was all I had. I knew my limits and they were reached. Whatever came next, I could die knowing I had done all that was possible on my part.

Dall screamed, ripping at his face. He tore away the knife as well as managing to open a few slash marks across his brow and cheeks.

"Kill him!" Dall screamed, struggling to deal with the pain and see me at the same time. He repeated what I assumed was the order in his own tongue. The Voy army at his back who had been standing sentry with their bugs moved their weapon to point at me.

I stood alone facing the Voy army. My whole body was a crisscross of open wounds and bruising to the extent I wasn't sure where one injury ended and the other began. My left eye was completely swollen shut.

"Who's next?" I asked, barely able to stand.

I caught motion from my left and right.

Cassie came to stand next to me. She placed one arm over my shoulder and the other arm in front of her, extending her shield to protect us both.

I felt like I could fall into her. Without her support, I probably would have.

"Come on, then!" Echo roared as he took his spot next to me.

Sam extended her hands. Angel and Preacher were on my right, the latter with this gleaming red cane sword in hand.

"You want one of us, then you come for all of us!" Preacher roared past the sands of the mobilizing Voy army.

All around us, what remained of our forces rallied for one last stand. The few mechs that still stood intact took up their positions on the frontline.

Loud cracks of thunder ripped through the night sky. I tilted my head upward to see an impossible sight. What looked like white lightning tore a hole in the space above us.

Circular gateways began to form, expanding out at the center. Black space on the other ends of the gateways gave way to ships as Galactic Government vessels poured through.

And not just the GG; a pair of dark green dropships bearing the Reaper sigil of the black scythe on a dark green background came through as well.

Dall and the Voy army looked on in awe with the rest of us.

"You bought us the time we needed." Madam Eternal sounded exhausted. "The Relic has been read. The book has been opened."

Galactic Government dropships that were still a day out from coming to our aid were somehow transported via a gateway through space to come to our aid. They were just as surprised as we were. The channels were going crazy as everyone tried to figure out what was going on.

I heard Colonel Strife coordinating with the Galactic Government.

One voice cut through above the rest. X being X decided to open a channel to that friendly tone.

"Daniel Hunt, you here? It's Papa. You remember Papa and the Reapers? Where you at, boy?"

"Papa," I managed to say with a grin that hurt. "Papa, it's good to hear from you. I'm on the frontline."

"Well, of course you are," Papa said with a smacking sound that I guessed was him slapping his belly. "I never been around so much GG in my life. Usually, we're running away from them, but this is a special occasion."

Dropships let off soldiers all around us as ground units rallied to our position. The Voy on their part were rushing to form lines with their artillery behind the bugs in front and the Voy soldiers between.

Shadow Praetorian units, the crack soldiers of the GG, positioned themselves to our right. The pair of Reaper dropships to my left flew low and slow to the ground. From their rear hangar bays, a series of vehicles roared out loaded down with Reaper warriors and weapons.

Ragtag vehicles that the Reapers used back on Earth maneuvered around the battlefield. It was a sight to see as ranks were formed on our end and orders were shouted. Shoulder to shoulder, we stood together, mercenaries, GG Praetorians, and Reapers.

"Man, you know things have really gone to crip when humans aren't fighting each other anymore," Papa said as he rolled up next to me in a dune buggy. He wore goggles and a vest that provided absolutely no cover but exposed his big belly. He carried a blaster in each hand with a toothy smile. "Boy, Danny, you don't look so hot."

"Yeah," I said with a smile despite the pain I felt. "Don't feel so good either. But it's great to see you. Thanks for coming."

"Once a Reaper always a Reaper." Papa touched the bone scythe at his neck that hung on his necklace. "We owe you big time. With that first dropship you got us, we managed to capture another. We're a force to be reckoned with now in the Badlands."

"Can you two save the catching up for another

time?" Captain Zoe Valentine asked, jogging up to me. "We have a war to win."

I'm not sure what came over me, but I managed to move one foot in front of the other and stand on my own power. I was finding reserves of strength I didn't know I possessed until now.

Cassie stayed close beside me as if she felt as though I could fall over at any moment. I might.

The Voy were working themselves into a frenzy again. I couldn't see Dall, but what I did see showed me the fight was far from over. Up and down the lines, Voy soldiers began injecting themselves with the super serum turning their bodies into the same abominations Dall had become.

"One more time!" Preacher bellowed. "One more time we break them here! We break them now!"

I was glad he took point on the epic battle speech. It was all I could do to look around for a weapon in the sand.

"Here." Echo pressed a blaster into my right hand. "Ready to ride the lightning one more time?"

"One more time," I answered.

Howls, war cries, "arrohhs" from the GG and those gathered lifted to the sky as one. In a united voice, humanity roared into the void, letting all who would oppose us know we would not go gently.

To this day, I'm not really sure if there was an order given to charge, someone got an itchy trigger finger and fired early, or something else, but before I knew it, both ranks of soldiers surged toward one another.

Not to be outdone, I tapped into the newly found reservoir of strength and ran with the first line at the enemy.

My left arm was beginning to heal. I found I could move it, albeit painfully at best.

I clashed with the first wave of Voy and the rest was a blur of reacting to threats without thinking.

Cassie and the rest of the pack rallied around me in the center of the fight, understanding I was less than equipped to enter the battle. Angel also kept an eye out for Preacher, who wove in and out of battle wielding his glowing crimson sword like the master he was despite his condition.

As the battle raged on, the comm line was a panic of voices, orders shouted and received. X did an amazing job keeping me connected with the latest reports shifting through all the comm lines and allowing me to hear what was most important in that moment.

"All Galactic Government units in the air: punch a hole through the enemy ships and target artillery," Colonel Strife shouted to his comrades.

"Understood. Dreadnaught One and Two on the way," a female voice I didn't recognize answered.

When I looked up into the sky, I saw a pair of battle class star cruisers making a turn for the Voy.

The ships were beyond impressive. Giant steel

beasts of war loaded down with rail guns, lasers, and who knew what other cutting edge technology the GG was developing came to bear on the Voy.

Each battle class star cruiser was shaped like ships of old that actually traveled on Earth's water. They were tall with a wide flat top and as long as ten city blocks.

Thrusters to their rear and on their underbelly kept them in the air.

To combat this new threat, the Voy were forced to send what ships they had left along with their artillery at the GG.

"Make 'em pay!" someone shouted on our side as the GG unloaded on the small Voy crafts trying to intercept them.

I almost felt sorry for the Voy trying to go kamikaze on the GG ships, almost. The Voy were cut down by barrages of fire from the star cruisers. The exchange with the artillery on the ground didn't go much better.

The desert floor quaked as the GG unleashed holy hell on the Voy artillery.

For the first time, I saw real fear in the eyes of the Voy.

"Here now!" I yelled in my exhausted numbed state. "Here! Now! We break their spirit!"

Everyone sensed the same thing I did. Winning, for the first time, was within our grasp. That crazy son of a brum Papa sent out a war cry and urged his Reapers forward. They slammed into the right flank of the Voy with their rusted vehicles and mismatched weapons.

Not to be outdone, the Shadow Praetorians gained ground on the left. The Coalition of Corporations I led went right up the gut.

As much as I searched for Dall on the battleground, he was nowhere to be found. No doubt he had already turned tail and run when he saw our reinforcements arrive.

"More portals are opening from the Relic," Wesley said over the comm. "Madam Eternal, who else did you call?"

"No one." Madam Eternal's voice came back slow and forced as if she barely had the strength to speak.

"We're getting reports of more allies with blue wings and purple armor joining the fight," Wesley said.

"There are other worlds than these," Madam Eternal answered. "Perhaps allies from a different place."

"As long as they're fighting the Voy, I think we can abide them," Julian answered. "But the Relic must be closed. It comes with a cost we will have to pay back in the future. Best not to dig ourselves a hole we won't be able to get out of."

"Agreed," Madam Eternal answered.

More chatter on the comms went on, but I had to concentrate on what was happening around me. We were on the verge of victory.

The Voy bugs lifted off into the sky trying to protect their artillery from the GG Dreadnaughts above. They were cut down like the rest.

The Voy soldiers on the ground turned tail and ran, to the roaring cheers of our forces. Oxygen came into my lungs, ragged and burning.

The red sun over Mars was just descending when the fighting stopped.

"We going after them?" Sam asked to my left.

"You can let the GG take it from here," Colonel Strife answered. "We'll harass them all the way back to their mountain fortress. No doubt that's where they're headed now."

As much as I would have liked to finish the Voy there and then, I had nothing left. Sweat trickled down my face, mixing with the blood both new and dried. My arms hung by my sides feeling as though they weighed a metric ton each.

Numbness crossed my body to the extent that I couldn't feel much physically or emotionally, for that matter.

"You going to make it?" Preacher asked, limping to my side. He had placed his red sword back into its sheath, using it as a cane once again. "You look how I feel."

We surveyed the landscape around us littered with bodies, bullet casings, and charge packs.

"I think so," I answered. "We did it."

"We almost did it," Preacher corrected. "The Voy'll make one last stand in that mountain fortress of theirs. Maybe even try to escape, but the GG will keep them in check."

"So much killing," I said, forcing myself to see the many bodies of our own as well as the enemy. "You think death will always follow us like this?"

Preacher knew exactly what I meant.

"I think we all have our burdens to bear in this life," Preacher said slowly. "I think we're uniquely equipped for the job."

"I've got to go find him," Angel said, popping into sight right next to us. If I had more energy, she would have scared me coming out of nowhere like that. An anxious panic lived in her eyes. "Jax, he's out there lost to that animal that lives inside of him. I've got to go find him."

"We will," Cassie said, moving to join us. "We'll find him, but you don't have to do it alone. You have allies now."

"What are you talking—"

Cassie cut off whatever Angel was going to say next with a raised finger. She removed her helmet, showing a sweaty brow and tired eyes. She placed her right finger to her ear. "Julian, we have a member that's missing. How long until we can get our ships to do a flyover around the surrounding area?"

We all stood silent for a moment.

"Got it, two minutes," Cassie answered with a weary nod. She looked at Angel. "They'll find him. They'll find him a lot faster in the air than we could on the ground. He's going to be okay."

Tears welled in Angel's eyes, and then in a very unlike Angel way, she actually went over and gave Cassie a hug.

I could see Cassie's athletic body tense at first as Angel approached her and wrapped her arms around her. A moment later, her body relaxed and she hugged Angel back.

"Thank you," Angel said as she released the woman.

Without another word, Angel swallowed hard then moved away to wipe her tears.

The end was near, but this wasn't over yet.

# TWENTY

THE REST of the night went by quickly with a trip back to the staging area, food, and sleep in the Pack Protocol tent Cryx erected for us.

Butch whined and nuzzled me nonstop when I arrived. Cryx looked at us with an open mouth then jumped into action, directing us where we could clean and where the food was she had prepared.

All I wanted to do was nothing, but robotically, I went through the acts of bathing and eating.

When sleep came, I dreamed of blissful nothingness.

When I woke the next morning, my body was free of wounds and soreness, thanks to my healing ability. But as always, my stomach growled, empty and hollow.

"You're like a bottomless pit," I said to my stomach,

swinging my legs out of bed, almost hitting Butch. "Oh, sorry, girl."

Butch got to her feet, looking at me expectantly, then stretched.

"I'm hungry enough to eat a Voy on super soldier serum right now," I said to X.

"Too soon," X answered. "If I never see another Voy again, it'll be too soon."

"What's the latest news?" I asked her.

"The GG harassed the retreating Voy back to their mountain fortress as we expected. Their numbers are cut to a fraction of what they once were," X reported. "Our forces are planning a final assault on the Voy right now."

"I want to be there to see it all end," I told her, throwing on a clean shirt and pair of pants left for me by who I guessed was Cryx. "Let's get some food and get going."

"I—I didn't know if you were coming back," Cryx told me like she was confessing something to me as I exited my small section of the tent. The young woman who I still saw as a girl brought me a steaming cup of caf. "I was listening in on a comm line to what was happening out there. Did you fight the whole Voy army by yourself?"

"Not by myself; it was just one Voy to buy us time," I answered, accepting the cup with a grin of thankfulness. "Thanks for the caf. You read my mind. Hey, how were you listening in on the comm lines anyway?"

"Oh—you know." Cryx shrugged, looking around at Sam, who had exited the shower and stood with us in the little sitting room in the tent. "Hey, Sam, you need some food?"

"Hey," I said wearily. "Did you steal a radio from someone?"

"More like borrowed," Cryx said with a shrug. "I already returned it."

Butch cocked her head to the side to take in Cryx as if to say, "Really now?"

I let it go, filling a plate at the table in the center of the room that was loaded with food. I took the approach of only having to make one trip, piling my plate high with as much as it could fit. I recognized all the food and wanted it all. From yogurt, meat, eggs, and cheese; I didn't discriminate. It was all fair game.

"I heard reports of other gates opening in the sky when the GG arrived." Sam picked up the conversation, filling her own plate. "Madam Eternal said two others opened. And did I hear that right? There was someone or something with blue wings and purple armor?"

"I didn't see them if there were." I shrugged, thinking about the possibilities of what the Relic really was, if it could be used again, and more importantly, if Julian was right, what price we would have to pay for using it at all. "Maybe I should have a talk with Madam Eternal before we head out again."

"Might be a good idea," Sam said, sitting in a chair across from me. She wore a white robe, her wet hair in a towel. "I'm onboard to see the final fall of the Voy, but I need to get back home to my family soon."

"I know," I said, thinking fondly of Sam's daughter and even her husband. They were good people in a galaxy empty of such. "You can go whenever you want. We can handle the Voy from here."

"No, I started this and I want to finish," Sam said, biting into a forkful of egg. "Thank you for that push, by the way. I mean, to use my abilities."

"What abilities do you have?" Cryx came and sat with us. Her eyes were twice their normal size. "Hey, you think if I could get my hands on some of this serum Immortal Corp used on you, I could be a super soldier too?"

"No!" Sam and I both said at once.

"Geez, it was just a question," Cryx grumbled. "But seriously, Sam. What can you do?"

I eyed Sam, wondering how she was going to respond. It was one thing in life to do something hard. It was that much harder to actually open up and admit to yourself it really happened and talk about it.

Sam chewed her food, slowly buying time. I could see the muscles in her jaw clench and unclench.

"I can move things with my mind," Sam finally answered.

"Whhhhhhhat?" Cryx said, looking at me for consensus then back to Sam. "That's so cool; what does it feel like?"

"It feels like—it feels like a part of me was woken," Sam answered thoughtfully. "It felt freeing to accept that part of myself instead of trying to bury it down deeper."

"That's amazing." Cryx nodded along with Sam's words. "You're a hero. You all are. The comms were going off nonstop about how the Pack Protocol members held back the Voy when the dunes fell. How you were all in the center of the fighting from the beginning."

I shifted, uncomfortable in my seat with all the praise. I didn't want it. I didn't do it for that reason.

I stood up barefoot on the ground ready to serve myself another plate of breakfast food.

Butch jumped to her feet, wagging her tail. She looked to the entrance of the tent and whined expectantly.

Cassie pulled back the curtain to the tent a moment later. She hesitated, looking at Sam in her robe. "Sorry, it's not like I can knock."

"Come on in." I waved her over. "How're you feeling?"

"Sore," Cassie said, entering our tent with a wince as she rotated her shoulders. "I don't heal like you do."

I looked Cassie up and down. She was once again dressed all in black with a long black cloak and deep set hood that tumbled behind her. Her hair fell on either side of her face.

*Stop checking her out,* I told myself in my mind. *This isn't the place or time.*

The truth was I found myself admiring Cassie more and more, not just for her poise on the field of battle, but for how far she'd come in her own life and her resolve to keep moving forward.

"We having breakfast?" Echo said, exiting his small squared off sleeping area. "Nobody told me."

Echo was a sight to behold. Instead of opting for a shower last night when we got in, he had opted for stuffing his face and passing out in his cot. He wore the black tight-fitting synth suit covered with sweat and dirt. Hands were black with grime and his face and hair didn't look much better.

"You really need a shower, man," I told him, unable to keep a straight face. "Like, bad."

"Shower before more food," Sam instructed like an older sister admonishing her younger brother. "Don't make me lift you up with my mental ability and place you in the shower."

"Ha!" Echo barked with laughter. "I didn't think

about that. Can you at least toss me a protein pack with your mind powers? I can eat while I bathe."

We all looked at Sam.

Sam concentrated on the table. A fist-sized protein pack lifted from the table and glided over to Echo, who snatched it out of the air.

"Sweet," Echo said, heading for the shower that was curtained off just like our sleeping quarters.

"So awesome," Cryx breathed.

"Daniel, may I speak with you for a moment?" Cassie asked.

"Sure," I said, sipping on my caf.

Cassie gave me a half amused, half deadpan stare.

"Uh, Daniel?" X prodded in my head.

"Oh, you mean in private," I said, placing my food and cup down. "Let me grab my boots."

I ran to my cot and the clean boots Cryx had left for me, lacing them quickly.

I exited the tent with Cassie.

The morning air was cold and new. The day had just begun, but the tent city that acted as our staging ground had never ceased to be alive with motion. Even now in the early hours of the morning, there were soldiers, mercenaries, and even Reapers trotting to and from errands.

"Walk with me?" Cassie asked.

"Lead the way." I extended a hand forward, only now realizing Butch had joined us.

We were getting looks of awe at the large wolf who jogged alongside of us sniffing at the cool air with her long snout.

Cassie and I made our way through the tents in a comfortable silence. I could tell there was something she wanted to bring up but was searching for the right way to do it.

"Is it Jax?" I asked.

"No, the Order is out searching for him," Cassie answered. "They'll find him now that it's morning. He'll be easier to track. It's the Relic."

"You and Julian want it back from Madam Eternal?" I asked, looking at our trajectory. The path we were taking led us to her small red tent. "Or if not you and Julian, at least Julian and the Order."

We stopped in a few tents down from Madam Eternal's. Cassie looked at me, searching my eyes so deeply, it was almost uncomfortable.

"I don't know what's going to come after all of this." Cassie took in the tents and hustle and bustle around us. "It's wonderful that we've all come together now, but the Voy'll be gone by tonight. Then we'll be back fighting amongst ourselves. I'm going to be honest with you now because I know who you are and I know I can trust you."

The heaviness in her words gave me pause.

"The Relic shouldn't be in anyone's hands. I see that now," Cassie said, biting her lower lip. "The Order,

Madam Eternal—no one should have it. A weapon like that, that can open portals between space is dangerous. Imagine being able to relocate an army from point A to point B in a matter of minutes? What if it got into the wrong hands?"

"And Julian believes there's a price to pay when these Relics are used," I said, remembering his warning. "How many Relics are there? Are they all books? Do they all do the same things?"

"If you believe the information the Order has passed down from generation to generation, then no, they're not all books, their number is unknown and they possess different powers," Cassie explained. "What matters right now is that you keep the Relic safe."

"Me?" I took a step back, shaking my head. "Why me? I don't want it."

"And that's why you're the perfect person to lead and protect the Relic," Cassie answered. "You're someone all parties involved will trust. If you don't, I'm afraid Julian will take it by force."

"Or he'll try and take it by force," I corrected, thinking back on the power Madam Eternal showed on the battlefield.

"Or he'll try and take it," Cassie agreed.

"I'll talk to her," I answered, seeing the position we were all in at the moment. "We'll talk to her right now."

Cassie nodded, falling in step as we crossed the space of the last few tents to Madam Eternal's.

Madam Eternal's tent was blood red with the sigil of a dragon. Her corporation was one of the smaller ones, but one which everyone respected. It was due to her healing abilities that many of the corporations' members were still alive today.

I was about to announce ourselves at the tent since knocking wasn't really an option. Before I had the chance, Butch let out a low, deep growl.

Something large shifted inside the tent, pressing against the tent walls, more slithering than walking.

# TWENTY-ONE

BUTCH LET out a series of savage barks. I took a step back, regretting not always carrying a weapon on me. When was I going to learn? Cassie, on the other hand, was always prepared. From her right forearm, two blades sprouted like claws.

Whatever it was inside the tent stopped moving.

"Madam Eternal?" I shouted into the tent, remembering her real name. "Carly, are you in there?"

"Yes, please come in." Madam Eternal appeared at the entrance of her tent, a moment later pulling back the fold that acted as a door. She looked down at Butch, who gave her a dirty look and a snarl. "Sister Wolf, why must we be at odds? I intend no harm to your master."

Butch huffed and snorted but stopped growling.

"What was that?" Cassie asked, sheathing her blades with a short metallic sound.

"What was what?" Madam Eternal said, looking at Cassie as if she really had no idea what she was talking about.

"There was something inside your tent." Cassie lifted an eyebrow. "Who or what is in there with you?"

"It's just me." Madam Eternal shrugged. "Please come in."

Despite my better judgment, I entered the tent with Cassie and Butch following behind. As soon as I entered, I was hit with a sweet smell in the air, something like orange and vanilla.

Unlike my own tent, which was sectioned off into smaller areas, Madam Eternal's was one large open area with a bathtub in the back right corner and pillows and blankets on the ground in the middle.

"You were right to call me by my true name," Madam Eternal said, motioning us to sit down on the ground amongst the pillows and blankets. "Friends should address one another without titles whenever possible and out of the eye of the public. Of course you're here to talk about the Relic."

Madam Eternal said it so matter-of-factly and without argument, I almost felt like this was going to be easier than I thought.

"Yes, but while we're here, since we're amongst friends, I thought I might be able to get a few more answers," I said hopefully, taking a seat on the floor next to Cassie and Butch. "What you did during the battle with the Voy. The way you shielded yourself from their weapons and the energy that came from your hands. What is it? How did you do it?"

"There is a lot to unravel in there," Madam Eternal said, sitting across from us on her knees. "An easy answer is magic, but think about this. To primitive man who first inherited the Earth while it still thrived, would not a flying vehicle or any vehicle at all be unexplainable to them? How about a blaster? They would interpret it as death wielded from a hand and they wouldn't be wrong."

"So what you're not telling us is that what you use is a kind of advanced science not yet discovered," Cassie asked, trying to follow along. "So how have you been able to understand and harness whatever this is and no one else has?"

"Someone else has," I said, thinking out loud back to the man called Nemesis. "The Galactic Government has found a way as well."

"Harnessing energy starts here," Madam Eternal said, touching her head. She rolled up the wide sleeves of her red robe to reveal what looked like a series of thin metal circuits on her forearms. "Channeling the energy here and tapping into dimensions that exist outside of our own."

"You're playing with fire," Cassie said in a hard tone. "Alternate dimensions, traveling through space; you cannot expect to understand it all."

"We're all students for the duration of our lives," Madam Eternal rolled down her sleeves. "But more than answers now, you want the book, the Relic."

"It shouldn't be in anyone's hands," Cassie said. "How Mordred held on to it all these years without it affecting him is something I still don't understand."

"Maybe it did affect him," I thought out loud, remembering the pale complexion of the man.

Madam Eternal drummed the fingertips of both hands against one another. She studied us, not in a combative way but truly thinking of a solution that would placate all sides.

"What would you suggest?" she asked Cassie and me. "The Order would destroy it. I cannot allow that to happen. You have seen its worth. It saved the human race from annihilation and slavery from the Voy."

"Daniel should protect it," Cassie answered. "As much as I would love to take it to be guarded by the Order, there are those amongst us that would rather it be burned. I, too, see value in what it did yesterday."

"I concur, then," Madam Eternal reached behind her to a pillow at her back and slid out the ancient tome. Without pause, she handed it to me. "Guard it well, Daniel Hunt. We may need it again in our lifetime."

I accepted the book with a new respect for the volume. There was real power within its covers that I had seen firsthand. A part of me wanted to open it.

Another part of me wanted to hide it away somewhere safe and never see it again.

"There were reports of other gateways being opened, across the battlefield," I said, placing the book in my lap. "Reports of other warriors or fighters from who knows where helping us against the Voy."

"The Relic promises aid from allies willing to help," Madam Eternal said. "All I know is that these warriors exist in our own universe. They were called, answered that call, then returned to their own homes. You may be required to return that favor in the future."

"There's always a cost when a Relic is used." Cassie spoke softly as if she were repeating some ancient proverb she had learned long ago. "The Order teaches us that early on. I just hope the price we must pay for using it this time isn't too steep."

The tent silenced. Even Butch who had been sniffing the pillows and blankets on the ground stopped.

"I hate to break up this lively moment, but Colonel Strife and Wesley are asking that you join them for a meeting," X said in my head.

I nodded slightly, letting X know I heard her and understood without breaking the silence.

I slowly rose to my feet with the Relic in my hands. The book was heavier than I remembered or maybe that was just what my mind was telling me. Something as rare and powerful as this needed to be protected and hidden away. Cassie was right.

"I have to get going," I said as Cassie, Butch, and Madam Eternal also regained their feet, sensing a close to the meeting. "Thank you for making this easy."

"Yes," Madam Eternal said, picking up a datapad next to her. The small screen shone bright. "I've been called to the meeting as well. And you're welcome. I'll be along shortly. I must see to something first."

That was enough for me. I had no desire to be inside the woman's tent any longer. I didn't think Madam Eternal was someone I had to worry about stabbing me in the back, but neither did I think she was safe.

We left the tent, Butch practically running to get out. When we were a safe distance away, Cassie let out a long, pent-up breath.

"Jeez," Cassie said, shaking her head. "That woman gives me the creeps. Maybe that's not even the right word for it. It's like there's so much more going on with her than meets the eye."

"I know what you mean," I said, gripping the book in my hands tightly. "I'm going to drop this book off with someone I trust and get it somewhere safe."

A rogue idea crossed my mind and I stopped three tents down from the Pack Protocol's tent. I handed the book to Cassie.

"Here, if you don't mind, can you give this to

Preacher? I'd like him to take it back to Dragon Hold," I offered. "It'll be safe there and Bapz can put it under the protection of the house."

"No, not me" Cassie shied away from the offered book with open palms. She pushed it back toward me. "What are you doing?"

"There's not a whole lot of people in this world that I trust," I said, looking down at Butch. "And Butch doesn't have opposable thumbs, so I can't really give it to her."

"Preacher is a better choice," Cassie said, motioning us both forward to the tent. She looked at me with wide eyes half full of disbelief, half full of gratitude. "Thank you, but I don't want it."

"And maybe that's exactly why you should take it," I said out loud. "Isn't that what you said to me about leading the corporations?"

"I knew that was going to come back to bite me in the butt," Cassie said with a wry smile. "All right, but you're coming along and then we can both go to the meeting."

Cassie accepted the book and took the lead back to the tent.

Preacher was just limping out of the black tent when we arrived. The older man looked the worse for wear. He relied heavily on his cane. He had entered the fight with the Voy at less than a hundred percent. The bruising and cuts across his face and hands made it clear he had only sustained more injuries.

A grin appeared on Preacher's face then quickly disappeared when he saw what Cassie held. He stared at the book with a deep sense of respect in his one good eye.

"Just taking an early morning stroll with a text of ancient power, are we?" Preacher asked, licking his dry lips. "Now why would you be coming to me with that?"

"Because you make the hard decisions when you have to and you stand by them," I told him, remembering what he had done for me when Amber died. He had made the decision to take me out of the equation then to save me from myself. "I told Cassie there's only a few people I trust. You two are among that number. Cassie can't really take off back to Dragon Hold without causing suspicion with the Order. It has to be you."

"And miss the final Voy encounter?" Preacher asked like it left a bad taste in his mouth. "I want to make those sons of brums bleed one more time."

"With the entire GG here, I think we'll be fine," Cassie said, offering Preacher the book. "Daniel's right. You're the right man for the job."

Preacher slowly took the book in his hand opposite his cane.

"Dragon Hold?" Preacher asked as if he already

knew the answer to the question and it was only a formality. "Bapz?"

"That's right," I answered. "The Hold is equipped with enough defenses to see it safe. Bapz will be able to guard and hold it, inside the grounds."

"I'll make sure it stays safe," Preacher promised, placing the book in a protective hold between his left arm and the left side of his body.

"I know you will, thank you," I said, turning to go.

Preacher headed back inside the tent while Cassie, Butch, and I made for the meeting tent, where Colonel Strife and Wesley waited.

"You have some good friends," Cassie said seriously.

"Not many of them, but yeah, I guess the ones I do have are—" Shouting coming from the white meeting tent reached our ears.

The pair of praetorians standing guard outside the tent rushed inside.

*You got to be kidding me,* I thought to myself as Cassie, Butch, and I broke into a run. *What now?*

# TWENTY-TWO

I BURST into the tent with Cassie a half step beside me. Butch was actually out in front.

Weapons were pointed in every direction. Papa stood with a butter knife in his hand, pointing it threateningly at Colonel Strife. Wesley stood in the middle with his hands extended toward either side trying to deescalate the situation.

The praetorian guards at the tent entrance lifted their weapons at Papa. Madam Eternal stood with her arms crossed and a raised eyebrow. Julian held the handle of his blaster at the small of his back.

"Wow, wow, wow, wow," I said, joining the chaos inside. "What's going on here? Papa, put down the butter knife."

"This GG elitist thinks he's better than me," Papa

said with wide, angry eyes taking in Colonel Strife across the table. "I think he wants a piece of Papa."

"I never said I was better than you." Colonel Strife took a deep breath, giving his praetorians the signal to lower their weapons. "I asked if you needed armor when we go meet the Voy for their surrender."

"I don't need your armor," Papa said, slapping his rotund belly, which stuck out of his vest. "I have all the armor I need right here. Five inches of belly fat, enough to stop any round aimed at me."

"Whatever you say," Colonel Strife answered, clearly done with the conversation.

"Papa, the knife?" I implored.

Papa looked at me then back to his extended right hand, which held the impromptu weapon.

"Daniel!" Papa said, a smile crossing his face. He lowered the knife and let it drop to the table in front of him. "Just a little misunderstanding; it's all good. It's all good."

"Right, so if we can get back to the matter at hand," Wesley said as the pair of praetorians moved to resume their guard at the entrance to the tent. "The Voy are requesting a meeting to surrender. They want you there, Daniel."

"Dall?" I asked, taking a guess.

"The one and only," Julian confirmed. "We didn't make their retreat easy. We captured as many of them as we could, but still a small group made it back to the safety of their mountain fortress. The GG bombed them all night. We received a transmission this morning from Dall. He said he'll surrender, but only to you."

"What are the odds that this is some kind of trap?" Madam Eternal asked from her place at the corner of the tent. "It wouldn't be the first time."

"Given their track record, I would say it's almost guaranteed it's a trap," Wesley answered. "We'll go in ready for a fight. One way or another, this all ends this morning."

"He shouldn't go," Cassie spoke up. "I mean, Daniel shouldn't go. Why would Dall want Daniel there? He hates him. He's not going to surrender to Daniel. He's going to try and kill him."

"Maybe," I said, struggling with the feeling that Cassie actually cared about me enough to voice it to an entire room. "But I'm not that easy to kill. I'll be all right.

Wesley said it. We need to end this now. One way or another. They can surrender or fight it out one last time, but it ends now."

"Commander Shaw was severely wounded in the fight. The Phoenix corporation will be sitting this one out," Wesley informed us. My face must have asked the question for me because Wesley added, "He'll live, but he's in no condition to engage the enemy at the moment."

"We've all sustained heavy losses," Julian agreed.

"That's why the GG will take the lead on this one," Colonel Strife chimed in.

"Oh no you don't, Fancy Armor," Papa said, using his new name for the colonel. "The Reapers spilt blood just like all of you. We'll be there too. Can't let the GG swoop in and take all the glory."

Colonel Strife opened then closed his mouth. I saw the muscle at his jawline twinge. I could make an educated guess that Colonel Strife wasn't used to being talked to in such a way.

"We will allow you to accompany us on the ground," Colonel Strife said, recovering quickly. "As a part of our overall strategy."

Papa looked like he was going to argue more.

"Well, that sounds like a great idea." I jumped into the conversation with a plastic smile and nodded with the plan. "Let's go then. We'll have the GG and Reapers on the ground in case anything goes wrong. I wouldn't have it any other way."

"As far as we can tell, there are only a few hundred Voy left," Wesley said, picking up the conversation before more arguing started. "Even if they do want to fight, it'll be over in minutes. We've wiped out their bugs, artillery, and aircrafts. We have them. There's no way out."

"We'll assemble our teams and meet in the staging ground for takeoff within the hour," Colonel Strife said.

"Within the hour, make sure you're ready at the staging ground," Papa echoed the colonel as if he had come up with the plan himself.

"Are you just repeating exactly what I said?" Colonel Strife looked over at Papa as he rose from his seat at the table.

"Just be there." Papa winked at the colonel.

We all left the tent, heading to pass along the word to our teams and prepare to leave.

Cassie, Butch, and I made for the staging ground.

"X," I said out loud. "Can you please tell the rest of the Pack what's going on and where to meet us?"

"You got it," X answered.

We entered the tent lined with gear and began donning our armor and weapons. Cassie kept on giving me a look that was one part hard stare, one part raised eyebrow, and one part pursed lips.

"I've got to go," I told her. "Even if it's a trap, and more than likely it is, we have them outnumbered and outgunned. We'll be all right."

"Well, I guess I'm not going to talk you out of it," Cassie said with a sigh. "I guess I'll have to be right next to you to make sure you don't get killed."

"I didn't know you cared so much about me," I said, buckling on my chest armor. "I mean—it's nice."

"Yeah, well don't let it go to your head," Cassie answered.

"Too late," I said, catching her eye. Before I could stop myself, I blurted, "I care about you too."

For the first time since I had known the woman, Cassie actually blushed. She turned her eyes from me and focused on clipping on her shoulder armor.

"Smooth," X said in my head. "Got to keep going now or we're just going to live in awkward silence."

"Will you just give me a minute," I whispered harshly.

"What's that?" Cassie asked.

"No, not you," I said, looking around the tent. The structure was wide and long. There were other soldiers there gearing up, but no one within close proximity. I steeled myself. "Cassie, when this is all over. I mean, after this morning when we get back. I mean, not right after we get back, but maybe tonight or tomorrow or something—"

"Ugh, this is so painful," X groaned in my head.

"Cassie, would you go out with me?" I asked.

Cassie's eyes went wide. "Like on a date?"

"Oh great, there's two of them," X said. "What are the odds she wouldn't be good at this either?"

"Yes, like on a date," I said, clearing my throat and forcing myself to keep eye contact. "If you want. If you don't—"

"Yes," Cassie said, cutting me off. "It's just I haven't been on a date since before my time with the Order. We don't really get out much."

"Yeah, you and me both," I admitted, trying to think back to any memory I had about going out on an official date. I came up blank. "What do people do on dates?"

"Eat, I think?" Cassie said, scrunching her brow in thought. "Maybe go see the latest holo film?"

We were saved from ourselves as Echo, Sam, and Angel found us in the tent.

The talk soon transitioned to proper gear, weaponry, and tactics, topics of conversation that I was much more familiar with navigating.

I found myself nervous and even excited, not for the meeting with the Voy, but on going out and getting to know Cassie better.

"Hey, Mars to Daniel." Angel broke me out of my train of thought. "Why do you have that stupid grin on your face?"

"I don't have a grin," I denied, holstering my MK II and remembering to clip two extra drums to my magnetic belt.

"Yeah, whatever," Angel answered. "Cassie told me the Order has a lead on the direction Jax is headed. I want to go find him. I mean, if it's okay with you."

"I'll go with you," I told her. "Let me finish this with the Voy and we'll find him together."

"No, he'll listen to me when he's like this, but anyone else, there's a chance he'll hurt." Angel's voice went from her normal rough and sarcastic, to soft for a moment. "I need to do this for him, alone. It has to be me."

"Okay," I said, looking past Angel toward Sam, who was showing Cassie and Echo a holo picture of her daughter and husband.

I realized then how much I cared for these people. They'd stood with me for years and came back to stand with me again through the worst of what the Voy had to offer. They had done enough. They had all done enough.

"You should go find him," I told Angel. "The GG and Reapers are more than the Voy can handle, even if they try something. You too, Sam, Echo."

All eyes swung in my direction.

"You've all done more than you had to," I said, looking them each in the eyes. I knew Cassie wasn't exactly a member of Immortal Corp. She'd have to come if Julian and the Order deemed it so, but I spoke to her along with the others anyway. "Go home, you're done."

"Well, thanks for the offer, but the Order and all..." Cassie shrugged with a smile. "I think I have to come."

"I got nowhere to go," Echo said honestly.

"Are you sure?" Sam asked. A wave of relief passed over her face whether she knew it or not. "I'll stay if you need me."

"No, go back and be a good mama to your family," I told her. "We got this."

Sam crossed the distance between us and hugged me so tight, I thought I was going to be crushed.

"Thank you," Sam said with tears in her eyes she quickly dismissed.

"No, thank you for coming," I told her.

"Of course," Sam said, already moving to say her goodbyes to the others. "We're family."

"I guess I'm going to take you up on that offer too," Angel chimed in. "I need to get to Jax as soon as possible and bring him back."

Echo opened his mouth to offer aid. Before he could get a word out, Angel extended a hand. "I can do this. I've done it before with zero casualties. Bringing anyone will just make the situation worse."

Echo closed his mouth.

The goodbyes were fierce and short.

Sam took Butch back to the tent on her way out. A possible ambush with the Voy was no place for the animal. I had to do something about that. I wondered if Bapz and X could come up with some kind of armor Butch could wear.

Butch kept taking a few steps toward the tent exit then looking back. Sam had to reassure her that I would be fine.

Soon it was just Cassie, me, and Echo in the tent.

"Here we go again," I said to the others.

"One more time into the belly of the beast," Echo agreed.

# TWENTY-THREE

THE RIDE to the mountain the Voy had chosen as their base of operation was uneventful. I got to see the true power of the Galactic Government first hand. Dozens of dropships accompanied the two battle class star cruisers.

The plan was simple. The star cruisers would open fire if the Voy tried anything in the air. On the ground, we'd go in with a thousand praetorians strong along with Papa and his Reapers.

If Wesley's numbers were accurate and there were only a few hundred Voy left, even if they wanted a fight, we'd overwhelm them. It was good to finally be on the side of numbers and artillery.

The dropships landed a few kilometers from the mountain. When we exited the Galactic Government dropship, I was surprised to see the Voy mountain and base in a smoking mass of destruction.

Apparently, the GG didn't mess around when it came to our species possibly being wiped off the face of the universe. They had brought all of the Voy buildings crumbling down around the Voy and most of the mountain.

The site was clear to see as well, meaning whatever camouflage technology that had hidden the site was destroyed in the bombing run.

Echo let out a low whistle.

"That's what I'm thinking," Cassie agreed.

The three of us stood in our armor as the praetorians and the Reapers assembled.

We all wore flat black armor and helmets. Cassie had her ebony cloak billowing behind her, the red cross symbol of the Order on her armor. Echo and I both carried the sigil of the wolf on our left shoulders.

MK II at my hip with my blade and axe at my waist, we waited for everyone to fall into place.

"Dall and Talia are obeying instructions thus far," Wesley said in my ear. "They've gathered their numbers right outside their destroyed base, no weapons that we can discern."

"How many?" I asked.

"Just shy of three hundred surviving Voy," Wesley answered. "Watch yourself."

"Will do," I answered.

"I'm patching you in to Colonel Strife in the air and Papa on the ground," X told me. "This all smells wrong, Daniel."

"No argument there," I said as Papa pulled up to me in one of his sand buggies the Reapers used on Earth.

"You know, this is my first time on Mars and I have to say I'm not a fan," Papa said, shielding his eyes against the midday sun. "Too flat and red."

"Red's not your color?" Cassie asked.

Papa answered by slapping an open palm on his rusted green buggy that carried the Reaper sigil, a scythe on the door.

"No, I like green. Not much of that on Earth these days, though," he said with a shrug.

"Phoenix is about to fix that as soon as this whole Voy mess is cleaned up," I reassured him. "Life will come back to Earth."

We piled into the buggy with Papa. A few Reaper vehicles, including motorcycles and quad riders, joined us. The Galactic Government made up the bulk of the convoy filling in our ranks until we were hundreds of vehicles moving along the desert ground.

The Galactic Government rode in a mix of hover tanks, troop transport trucks, and assault vehicles with large caliber weapons mounted on the tops of the roofs. It was clear the GG was taking no chances.

If the Voy did try anything, they'd have to be insane.

We saw the Voy on the desert terrain standing in

single-file rows waiting for us. They looked tired and defeated. Many of them had wounds wrapped in dirty bandages. I couldn't make out Dall as our forces made a rough semicircle around him, but I knew he was there. I could practically feel his hateful eyes boring into me. Red dust kicked up all around us as we came to a stop. I hopped off.

"This'll be your show," Wesley told me. "Colonel Strife is in the air if anything goes wrong. Papa and the rest of the GG have orders to kill with malice if the Voy spring an ambush."

"Understood," I said, crossing the space between our forces with Cassie on my left and Echo on my right. The former was able to bring a shield up with her forearm and a blaster in the other. The latter carried a heavy assault repeater, barrel to the ground, for the time being.

I could see our own forces with weapons pointed at the Voy. Itchy trigger fingers from praetorians who hadn't seen enough fighting yet to know they wanted no part of it worried me.

All it took was a single round to be expelled by accident to set this party off. I had to finish it before anything could go wrong.

I stopped twenty meters from the front of the Voy lines, still looking for Dall and not finding him.

"Well, here we are," I said out loud through my

helmet. "Dall wanted me here to surrender, so let's get this done."

The Voy ranks parted to let through not one figure but two. The first Voy that approached me limped, half her face scarred from what I guessed was the result of a GG bomb dropped on their fortress. Talia tried to stand tall and regal, but it was clear to see every movement for her was painful.

Dall came next. The behemoth wore a bandage around the eye I had taken from him with my knife. Thanks to his change at the hands of the super soldier serum, he was still tall and bulky, his skin covered in those hard rock-like scales.

They both stared daggers at me.

"How's that arm of yours I broke?" Dall asked.

"It healed faster than I thought," I said, rolling around my shoulder, testing it for discomfort. "That eye of yours, though. I don't think it's coming back. That serum made me heal quick; it just made you into more of a monster than you already were."

Dall clenched his fist so tight, his entire hand and arm shook with rage.

"We're not here to exchange insults," Talia said. "We're here to end this!"

What happened next was a blur of motion. My instincts were fast and my reflexes razor sharp, but in the millisecond it took for me to see both Talia and Dall reach behind them for weapons, I knew I was going to be too late going for my own. Each Voy brought a weapon to bear on my chest, my own MK II a hair's breadth behind their own.

To my right and left, I could see Echo and Cassie also moving to action. If they would be able to fire on the Voy before they fired on us was yet to be seen.

Time took on a different pace as I saw the weapon first aimed then fired on me. Talia carried a smaller caliber weapon in a single hand. She squeezed the trigger in rapid succession.

I braced, ready for the pain as I returned her fire. My Mk II aimed directly at her skull.

The pain from the rounds Talia fired never touched me. Instead, Echo threw his body in front of mine, firing his own heavy blaster.

Talia's rounds struck Echo in his chest. Whatever the rounds were ate through his armor like acid.

Both my own round and Echo's slammed into Talia's face, penetrating bone and devastating brain matter. The Voy fell to the ground, dead.

Cassie traded fire with Dall, one arm calling her shield in front of her, the other sending a spray of blaster fire at his face.

Like Talia, Dall managed to get off a few rounds directed at me. Echo once more used his body as a shield, taking the rounds.

"Rawww!" Echo screamed in pain as he fell back into me. I supported him, turning him to the side to shield him with my own body as I poured rounds into Dall's hardened skin.

Cassie closed the distance between them, quickly trading out the function of her augmented right forearm from blaster fire and using the twin blades instead.

As much as I wanted to go and help her, I knew Echo needed more in that moment.

All around us, the remainder of the Voy surged forward to meet our own Galactic Government and Reaper forces.

I sank to my knees, not caring about the outcome of the fight around me. Instead, I looked at Echo. I knew he was going fast even before I took off his helmet.

Talia and Dall were aiming for me. They knew exactly what I was and how to neutralize my healing ability. Echo didn't heal as quickly as I did. Whatever rounds struck his body were laced not only with acid but with the toxin used on Preacher that inhibited our ability.

Echo's breathing came in long, shallow gasps. His chest was a mess. The rounds had already eaten through his armor, infected his body, and were working their way through his chest cavity.

Echo coughed, fumbling with his helmet.

I did what I could, which wasn't much. I helped him remove his helmet, propping him up to rest in my lap.

"Daniel—Daniel—I'm sorry." Echo's face was pale.

His eyes were full of manic tension, not at dying, but at dying without my forgiveness. "I—I—Amber, I mean. I—"

The rest of what he was going to say got cut off as his body spasmed. Blood spurted from his lips and trickled down the side of his mouth.

"He doesn't know," X reminded me. "He doesn't know the Order saved Amber and that she's alive and well. You need to tell him. Tell him and let him go peacefully. I scanned his body. He has a few seconds left. The toxin the Voy used inhibited his healing ability and has already eaten through major organs."

"Echo," I said, taking one of his hands in my own and squeezing it tight. "Echo, you listen to me right now!"

I didn't mean to shout, but I had seen death come for so many before that I knew he had seconds left. Echo's eyes were already beginning to glaze over. I needed him to focus one last time.

"Echo, I forgive you," I told him, staring him dead in the eye. "You didn't kill Amber. You tried, but the Order saved her. She's safe now living a normal life. She's married, happy, with a baby on the way."

I felt my own eyes tear up. I ripped off my helmet so he could see me. I had no shame of crying. I didn't care what anyone else thought. Not that anyone was looking at me to begin with. The battle raged around me, short lived but brutal. The Voy had already lost whether they knew it or not.

"She's alive?" Echo said, staring at me in wonder. Tears fell down his eyes freely, not of pain or fear, but of wonder and joy. "Amber's alive?"

I nodded, clenching my jaw. I barely got the next words out. "She's alive, brother. And so am I, thanks to you."

"We are brothers, aren't we?" Echo said, turning his gaze from me to the bright clear sky above. "You're my family."

"We are," I answered.

Echo died in my arms. He was my brother turned enemy and then family once more.

I'm not sure how long I sat there on my knees cradling Echo's head, but it couldn't have been long.

"Daniel?" X said quietly in my head. "Daniel, you did the right thing. He can go in peace now, but there are others here that still need you."

Gently placing Echo's head on the sand, I rose to my feet. There would be more time to mourn in the coming days.

Right now was a time to kill.

Sorrow deteriorated to fury, and rage consumed my heart.

# TWENTY-FOUR

THE VOY NEVER STOOD A CHANCE. The few soldiers they had like Dall were the only ones still on their feet after a heated exchange of weapon fire. All around the field of battle, the Galactic Government and Reapers took down the augmented soldiers with a combination of weapons fire to their faces.

It seemed the only soft spot they had were their eyes.

Cassie fought Dall one on one while I sat with Echo, but soon she was joined by Shadow Praetorians and even Papa himself, who fired ancient shotgun rounds into Dall's face.

By the time I arrived, Dall was already reeling from the amount of damage he had taken. His eyes were a mess of blood and gore.

Cassie was giving him all he could handle, leaping

and rolling around his would-be strikes. Dall screamed in frustration as she scraped her bladed weapon across his rock-hard exterior. Sparks flung into the sky on contact.

Dall managed to reach a few praetorians who got too close. The Voy tore into their armor and helmets, but his movements were slowing already. He was tiring.

Rage more than a clear plan clouded my judgment. I ran at him, abandoning all strategy or tact. I picked up momentum, sprinting over the terrain toward him as fast as my feet would carry me.

He had me in both size and height, but I was no ordinary man. I poured everything into my sprint, colliding with the monster Dall had become at a speed that took us both off our feet.

It felt like tackling a concrete barrier.

Oxygen was torn from my lungs as I landed on top of Dall's chest.

The recallers on my wrists brought my axe and knife to my hand on command. Dall's remaining good eyes stared up at me with malice.

He opened his mouth as if he were going to jerk his neck forward and take a bite out of my face.

"Bad idea," I said out loud as his open maw extended forward. Rows of teeth covered the inside of his mouth. I got to play dentist as I ripped my axe into his mouth and tore outward.

Teeth and blood sprinkled the air around me. I followed the act with my knife.

Dall screamed, realizing his eyes weren't his only tender spot, but the inside of his mouth as well. Soon his efforts to bite me turned into a frantic attempt to get me off of him. He clawed at me, with his hands raking my armor and face.

I felt white-hot pain rail around my skull as he landed a few blows and cut across my face and head.

No amount of pain was going to stop me now. Not after what he had done to me, to Preacher, to Echo. I saw red as I hacked away at his mouth and eyes. With each strike of my axe and knife, I let go of some of the pain I felt inside.

By the time I was done, I didn't remember if I had cut into him twenty times or fifty. My chest burned with the oxygen coming in short, ragged gasps. My arms felt heavy and numb.

I didn't realize why I had stopped before, but I knew why now. Cassie stood beside me with her hand on my right shoulder. She didn't say anything. Her grip was firm but not crushing.

I looked up at her.

I was covered from head to toe with the gore that had been Dall. Cassie still wore her helmet. I could see my own reflection in her visor.

I looked like an animal. Some kind of blood-soaked creature giving in to the blood lust of a kill.

I looked down at my bloody weapons and the area that used to be Dall's head. Not much was left besides portions of his skull. Teeth littered the ground everywhere.

"It's over," X said quietly in my head. "It's over, but Dall can still win if you don't rein in what you feel now. Don't lose yourself in this. Don't lose who you are. Who you want to be."

I understood everything X said and didn't say.

Like Jax would get lost to that animal instinct inside of us, I knew I, too, had the potential of doing the same.

I stood up from Dall's corpse for the first time, seeing that I had gathered a crowd. The fighting was over. Most of the Voy had been killed with a handful of captured that were too wounded to fight until their end.

No one said anything, but dozens of Reapers and GG praetorians looked at me with a mixture of horror and respect.

I'm not sure anyone had taken down one of the Voy's enhanced soldiers without support and heavy weaponry.

I didn't know what to say or if I even had to say anything. I was emotionally and physically drained.

"Come on," Cassie said, draping a tender arm over my shoulder. "Come on, let's go. It's over here. It's done."

She guided me like some kind of lost puppy through the crowd.

"The body, Echo's body," I managed to say over the cloud of rage that was just lifting past my vision. "I want to carry him back."

"All right," Cassie answered. "Okay."

We found him where I left him. His eyes were open, looking toward the sky overhead. His chest was a ruin of melted armor. But his face almost seemed happy, peaceful in a way I had yet to know.

"I got him," I said when Cassie tried to help me lift Echo. "Thank you, but I want to do this for him."

I carried him in my arms back to a dropship headed to return home. Papa met us at the rear hatch as I placed Echo gently inside.

"He was a good man at heart," Papa said, remembering his own brief interaction with Echo when we first managed to procure a dropship for Papa and the Reapers. "He was conflicted. Made bad choices but often good people do make those bad decisions. What matters is that they come back in the end."

I exchanged a confused look with Cassie, who had removed her helmet.

"I didn't know you were so insightful," Cassie told the Reaper.

"I have many layers," Papa said, slapping his belly. "I'm a complicated character myself."

The rest of the day was a blur. I took Echo's body

back to the base camp and then packed up that night and headed for Dragon Hold. I had no desire to be part of the circus when the reports came or the bureaucracy as the Galactic Government began cleanup.

I didn't want Voy tech like many of the other corporations present or any kind of compensation. I had never wanted any of it. All I wanted to do for the time being was put my brother to rest.

The very next day, I was back at Dragon Hold handing off the leadership role of being head of the unified corporations to Wesley, who was much better at these things than I.

The only thing that gave me a moment's hesitation about leaving was Cassie. I didn't know when I'd see her again. She promised to work something out with Julian and come visit me at Dragon Hold within the next day or two.

I woke the next morning in my bed at Dragon Hold with Bapz knocking at my door.

"Come in," I mumbled from my bed. I rolled over to get a view of the door.

Bapz entered with Butch on his heels. The latter trotted over to me and placed a massive wet tongue on my forehead like she was giving me some kind of blessing.

"Good morning, Master Hunt," Bapz said with a wide grin across his liquid metal face. "May I have breakfast or that caf you love so much brought to your room?"

"Sure," I said, sitting up in my bed. "And it's just Daniel. You don't have to call me Master Hunt."

"Right." Bapz smiled again. He hesitated for a moment as if he were debating telling me something or not. "Hypothetically speaking, if I had news to give you, would you prefer said news first thing in the morning or would you rather get dressed and eat?"

"Hypothetically speaking?" I asked.

"Hypothetically speaking," Bapz confirmed.

"I don't know how many more times we can repeat the phrase 'hypothetically speaking' to one another, but I'd rather have the news now," I said. "Go ahead, let me have it. What are we doing now? More aliens? Rival corporation out to kill us? Gangs from Earth going to make an assault on Mars?"

"No, no, no, nothing like that." Bapz came over to me and placed a cool metallic hand on my forehead. "Are you okay? You don't feel like you have a fever."

"I'm fine, just tired from all the killing and politics of it all," I said with a sigh. "But what's going on?"

Bapz removed his hand from my forehead, which was still sticky from Butch's drool. He looked at it with a grimace.

"Right," Bapz answered. "You actually had a call from a professor at the Phoenix Corporation who wanted to speak with you. She sounded like a young woman. She said her name was Doctor Warden."

Memories of my interaction with both Doctor Warden and her father, who we had saved from Immortal Corp, crashed through my mind.

"Did she say what it was about?" I asked. "Is she okay?"

"Oh yes, it didn't seem like an emergency, although I don't have details past what she told me," Bapz answered. "She just called this morning and asked if you might call her back when you woke."

"Thanks," I said, remembering Echo and the funeral that needed to take place. "Echo and—"

"X and I have coordinated and taken care of all the details," Bapz answered.

"We'll do him justice, give him a peaceful place to rest," X chimed in. "We've already contacted the Pack. We'll have it in a few days to give everyone time to get here."

"Right," I said, swinging my legs out of bed. I thought the shirt and short length underwear I wore were tame enough, but apparently, I was the only one. Bapz turned to go.

"I'll have food brought, and if you'd like, we can go over details of the funeral," he said over his shoulder. "There are other items that need to be addressed as well, but they can wait."

Bapz left me to my own devices dressing and washing up for the day.

"Hey, X," I said to the empty room.

"Yes," X answered.

"I wanted to say thank you for reminding me to tell Echo about Amber. I think he died peacefully."

"I would say he did as well," X agreed. "And you're welcome. Would you like me to make a call to Doctor Warden?"

"Yeah, if you could," I answered, rinsing my face in the bathroom and brushing my teeth.

X opened a comm link that beeped twice before a familiar voice on the other end picked up.

"Daniel, are you okay?" Monica Warden's voice reached me, stressed and worried. "I've been following all the latest reports. After Commander Shaw was wounded, I was out of the loop, only getting sporadic updates."

"I'm fine," I said, giving her an honest answer about my physical state. I didn't feel like spilling my guts and reliving Echo's death all over again in my mind. "What's going on? Are you okay?"

"Yes, more than okay," Monica answered. "We did it, Daniel. Despite the Voy invasion taking place and being dealt with, we've been hard at work on the super seed and bringing life back to Earth. We're ready to begin and we want you and Immortal Corp to be a part of this."

# TWENTY-FIVE

"DANIEL, DANIEL ARE YOU STILL THERE?" Monica asked over the line. "Did I lose you?"

"No, I'm still here," I responded. "But I think you're talking to the wrong guy. There's not really an Immortal Corp anymore or a coalition of companies. That was a one-time deal to take on the Voy. Infighting and business as usual are about to take over now. It's not all kumbaya around the fire."

"Well, whatever you think you're a part of right now, whatever you do, I want you to know you have a home at Phoenix," Monica said in a rush of passionate words. "Come work with us or bring your company or not company or whatever; we just want you to know you have a place here. We're going to be doing some amazing work on Earth, things that will shape the future, and we want you to be a part of it."

I stood, looking at myself in the bathroom mirror. I heard everything Monica was saying. I knew it was no coincidence that she had chosen to make the call to me now right after the Voy had been defeated. She was worried about what would happen to me.

The mirror image stared back without blinking. Average height, muscular without being bulky, short dark hair and eyes. But that was all on the outside. Inside, I was a killer. Born and bred to fight, and if I was honest with myself, I loved it.

Left to my own devices, I might go back to life as a mercenary or a gladiator on the moon. Sooner or later, the animal that lived inside of me would want out of his cage once more.

"Is this thing working?" Monica asked again. "Daniel, are you okay?"

*Someone's trying to reach out and save you from yourself,* I thought in my own head. *Someone cares and is smart enough not to throw charity your way but ask you to work on creating a better galaxy.*

"I'm in," I said without thinking about it a moment longer. "I don't know if it'll just be me or Immortal Corp or whoever, but I'm in."

X cleared her throat.

"Sorry, *we're* in," I corrected myself.

Butch barked in my room. The massive wolf came to the door to the bathroom wagging her tail.

"Daniel, do you have a dog now?" Monica asked.

"Not a dog; she's an extinct wolf that was brought back from the dead by a rich family," I answered honestly. "Wow, it sounds weirder when I say it like that."

"An extinct wolf brought back from the dead?" Monica repeated.

"We'll explain when we see you again," X answered for me. "We have a lot to catch up on."

"I believe it," Monica said. "Well, I know I speak on behalf of all of Phoenix when I say we're happy to have you on board."

Butch barked again.

"All of you," Monica added.

"I'll be in touch soon," I answered. "I have to finish a few things here first."

"Understood," Monica said. "If you need a place to stay, you know you have a home here."

"Thank you," I answered.

With that, the line went dead.

"Earth, huh?" X asked.

"Earth," I said with a shake of my head. "Hopefully, it'll be a nice, quiet mission. I mean, how bad can it be? We'll be planting super seed on Earth, right?"

"Do you really want it to be quiet?" X asked, already knowing the answer to her question. "I think we both know that even the best laid plans never go exactly how they're supposed to."

"I hear that," I said, leaving the bathroom.

There was a slight knock on the door.

"Come in," I said.

To my surprise, Bapz walked in with a tray loaded with breakfast food and caf.

"Usually, I'd just have someone else bring it for you, but I had another message to deliver to you as the keeper of Dragon Hold," Bapz remarked, placing the tray on a table.

"I hate to burst your bubble, but I don't think I'm going to be at Dragon Hold much longer," I said, picking up the hot cup of caf and blowing on the steam. "I've been hired to go to Earth to help Phoenix bring life back to the planet. I know Dragon Hold will be in good hands with you at the helm."

"Oh goody. Are we all going together, then?" Bapz looked at me with his steel smile, nodding along as if what he had just said made sense. "I'll have Dragon Hold up and ready to go by tonight."

"No, I think what we have here is a failure to communicate," I said, sipping on the caf then grabbing a fresh baked fruit bar off the tray of food. "I'm going. Dragon Hold is going to stay here on Mars."

"Oh right," Bapz said, snapping his fingers. "X didn't tell you?"

"Tell me what?" I asked. "X?"

"I didn't think it was my place to say, and to be honest, it didn't really make sense to me," X answered slowly as if she were reading something. "I'm looking at the schematics now and—am I reading these right?"

"Oh, you're reading it correctly," Bapz answered, extending his hands forward with both palms up. A holographic display image popped up, showing something my eyes saw but didn't understand.

What Bapz held was an image of Dragon Hold in his hands. More than just Dragon Hold, in fact. The main mansion structure and the surrounding grounds were included in the holographic display. I could see the man-made forested area in the rear. At the front, the bridge that headed toward the front gates. And it was all flying.

"I may have gotten hit in the head too many times," I said, wincing at the image in front of me. "Is —is Dragon Hold—I mean, the entire grounds... flying?"

"Oh yes." Bapz nodded emphatically. The shiny steel hair on his shiny head didn't move in the least. "When the Cripps family built Dragon Hold, they wanted the grounds to also act as a ship in case of emergency. More than just the manor itself, but the surrounding grounds as well."

"Rich people and their money," I said, shaking my head. I took a closer look at the thrusters propelling the mansion into space. "Is there a dome or something keeping the grounds protected?"

"Yes, in fact, Harold Cripps, Rose's father, was a

leading mind in the structural development of a new technology—"

"I'm just going to stop you there," I said, lifting a hand to Bapz. "I'm just going to pretend I understand if you explain everything to me. I'll save you the time. I just need to know that it can fly in space safely."

"Theoretically, yes." Bapz nodded with a smile. "It's never been tested, but all the simulations check out time and time again."

"Great," I answered. "So this'll be our maiden voyage."

Bapz nodded even more emphatically.

"I don't think there'll be an issue," X chimed in. "At least, not an issue that we can foresee at the moment. Inevitably, there will be something that goes wrong and we'll adjust to survive."

"Are you trying to make me feel better?" I asked.

"No, just stating the facts to give you the full scope of things." X paused for a moment. "You don't pay me to be a yes woman."

"I pay you?" I asked.

"Well, you should, now that you have over a billion credits in your account," X teased me. "I'll start with a vacation."

"I'm not arguing with you there," I answered. "Okay, so we figure out what becomes of Immortal Corp, we put Echo to rest, and we head to Earth. What could go wrong?"

"Don't ask," Bapz said with wide eyes as if he were still trying to figure out why I'd tempt fate in such a way.

"At the moment, Wesley is asking for a call," X informed me. "Should I put him through?"

"You had to ask," Bapz scolded as he bowed out of the room.

"Go ahead," I told X.

"Daniel," Wesley said over the comm line.

"I'm here," I answered.

"It's good to hear your voice," Wesley replied. "I know it's hard to talk business when Echo isn't even in the ground, but if we don't do something now, we'll have more problems, resulting in even more deaths."

"What's wrong?" I asked. "The Voy? Did we not get them all?"

"Oh, we got them all, all right." Wesley sighed and continued in a tired voice. "The GG are all over the place securing the Voy base and collecting alien tech. The other corporations are in a furious state. They think they should be allowed to take spoils of war for themselves."

"Yeah, I can't see the GG stepping aside while The Order or Madam Eternal walk into the Voy base and take what they want," I agreed. "Sounds like a political mess."

"You know it," Wesley answered. "Which leads me to the reason I called. Immortal Corp as we know it is dead. The Founders are dead or gone so deep into hiding, we'll never find them. But there are employees looking for leadership. Good people without jobs and lost as to what to do."

"I can't," I stated, walking over to the large window in my room. "I can't do it, Wesley. I know you want me to be the new head of Immortal Corp, but that's not me. Some things need to die and Immortal Corp is one of them. I'm sorry for all the people without a job, but that's not my responsibility."

"Okay, okay," Wesley uttered thoughtfully. "But hear me out. What if we do let Immortal Corp die. What if we bring them into a new corporation bent on helping instead of killing. The universe understands we're here to stay now. I'd imagine that there will be more visitors both friendly and hostile to come. What if the Pack Protocol lived on past the death of Immortal Corp?"

I stood silent, looking out onto the ground of Dragon Hold. In front of me, the long driveway to the bridge and then the gate greeted my eyes. I was still getting over the fact that the entire grounds could get into the air.

"I'm going to Earth to help Phoenix bring life back," I told Wesley. "If what's left of Immortal Corp is in line with that, I don't see a problem. But you manage the day-to-day business side. I'm not ready to take on that burden. I'd rather face down an army of swarming Voy than sit in a board meeting in a suit and tie."

"Deal," Wesley said. I could hear the relief in his voice. "We'll have to come up with a new company name. Hunt Industries or Hunt Corporation has a ring to it."

"Yeah, not so much," I said, thinking of my past. How could a kid from an orphanage climb so high to have his own company? It seemed like a dream, surreal in every way. "Come up with some more names and we can decide what to call ourselves later. I think right now that's the least of our worries. We have one of our own to bury."

# TWENTY-SIX

BAPZ ASSURED me that the cemetery on the grounds of Dragon Hold was deep enough to carry the bodies with us. Even when the thrusters took the grounds off Mars, the cemetery would be safe.

Dragon Hold was even more extensive than I'd thought. To the right rear of the manor was the man-made forested area that housed wolves given a new chance on life. On the left side was a simple sandy area in a perfect square. Headstones clearly marked it as a cemetery.

Unlike the cemetery I had been to when I was looking for Amber, this cemetery was more high tech. I should have known. It was part of the Cripps family grounds after all.

For the occasion, I made myself wear a black suit and tie. A white shirt hugged my body. I was aware the fabric was expensive and soft. None of that meant anything to me. Money would come and go. I understood happiness, true happiness came from within.

Unlike money, we would never get back time. And that was what Echo had run out of: time.

I arrived at Echo's grave before anyone else. As I walked past the rows of gravestones belonging to the Cripps family, I realized the headstones were more than just pieces of steel etched with the names of each family members' names and dates of when they were born and died.

Some kind of motion sensor detected when someone was close. A holographic display of a portrait of the person buried there popped above the headstone in a light blue light.

I passed the rows of graves seeing names I didn't recognize, and finally, one I did. Howard Cripps and Martha Cripps were buried side by side with a grave for their daughter Rose Cripps.

As I walked by, Howard's hologram image came to life as well as his wife's. Howard had been tall and gaunt. His face wasn't harsh, but there was no overt kindness in his eyes either. If I had to guess by looking at him, he was matter of fact and business-minded.

Martha Cripps appeared a moment later as I passed. This woman had fire in her eyes. A hint of a smirk lifted the corners of her lips as if she knew some kind of secret I didn't. I could see Rose had taken after her mother more so than her father.

Finally, Rose's hologram appeared over the steel headstone. The woman I met in the Voy prison then fought beside at the Way settlement stood in front of me with a raised eyebrow and a grin.

"Did you know what you were doing?" I asked her out loud. "Are you sure you made the right decision, giving me all of this?"

Of course Rose didn't reply. She just stood there staring at me. The eyebrow lifted, the smile on her lips.

"I think she knew what she was doing." Cassie's voice made me turn to look behind me. I hadn't heard her approach and that was saying a lot for my heightened hearing.

I didn't really know or care how I was supposed to say hi to her now. I crossed the space between us and wrapped her in a hug. Cassie embraced me with open arms. She wore a plain black dress, no jewelry or makeup.

I stood there not caring who saw us or what it all meant. It felt right. Cassie smelled like some kind of light perfume. It reminded me of spice on a clean morning breeze.

"Thank you for coming," I said, taking a step back sheepishly.

"You know I wouldn't miss it for all the Relics of the ancient worlds," Cassie said.

My eyes went large before shaking my head. "Too soon. If I never see another Relic in my life, I'd be good with that."

"Word is Immortal Corp is officially gone and that you're going to Earth to help Phoenix," Cassie said. "I wasn't going to get an invitation?"

"Can you?" I asked, half ashamed I hadn't thought of it before but half confused if that was even a possibility. As far as I knew, the Order had no ties to Phoenix or interest in aiding Earth's recovery.

"I proposed the idea to Julian. Said I was going to keep an eye on you and Phoenix as well as the Relic," Cassie said with a playful smile. "Julian's not a dummy. He knows what I really want, but he was okay with it. I think he sees the same thing I see in you."

"What's that? A friend who gets his own friends killed?" I commented before I could stop myself. I didn't even know I was carrying that guilt with me until I said it, but there it was.

"It wasn't your fault." Cassie came to me, placing her right hand on my forearm firmly. "Never think that. You had no idea or way of knowing that they'd attack with that weapon."

"I knew it was an ambush." I shook my head, swallowing hard. "I knew the Voy weren't just going to lie down. I could have gone alone. I should have gone alone."

"You did everything you had to do. Echo and I are

our own people, capable of making these decisions for ourselves. We both wanted to go and we did. He saw an opportunity to save you and did. That was his choice, his sacrifice. Don't you take that away from him. He earned that. He earned the right to take credit for his actions."

I slowly nodded.

I was half surprised I had even been carrying the guilt, but how could I not? When you're the leader, you're the one in charge of everything. He was my responsibility.

Before we could say more, people began to arrive. First Angel, back for the day from tracking down Jax, then Sam, who after a brief visit with her family, turned back around to attend the funeral. Preacher, Bapz, Wesley; they were all there, even Butch.

Bapz had seen that a clean steel block was brought and placed for Echo in the cemetery. Just like the others, a blue holographic display of Echo sat above the headstone.

He looked happy in the picture. I was grateful to Bapz for choosing such a flattering image of our friend. Echo stood with his arms crossed and a twinkle in his eye as if he were posing for some kind of modeling shoot.

He was alive, happy, and would remain so in that image for eternity. For the first time, I realized that the holographic images actually moved, not a lot but a little like a five-second video playing over and over again. I couldn't believe I had missed it at first.

Echo shifted and smiled at someone off camera as if they were sharing a joke.

Everyone in attendance wore black as was customary at a funeral. Cryx actually came, along with some of the members of the Way.

Wesley took a step forward to stand beside Echo's grave. He looked at each of us for a moment, thinking hard of the words he was about to use.

"When I recruited Echo to be in the Pack Protocol, he was just a kid. Well, I still think of him as a kid. He was more like a teenager at the time." Wesley looked to his right where the holo image of Echo grinned back at him. "He was a good kid. He just wanted to have a family and I think that's what he found with all of us. Loyal to a fault. Echo was a great friend at his core."

I thought about those words. Wesley was right. He was loyal to a fault. Even when he was given the order to kill Amber, his faithfulness to Immortal Corp first and then the Pack Protocol came into play. He had followed through on what he was told to do, loyal to a fault.

I really didn't want to say anything. I wasn't a fan of public speaking, and to be honest, I didn't know if I could get the words out. But Echo had taken the bullets meant for me. I felt as though I owed him a few words of thanks.

Wesley stepped to the side, reaching for a cigar from his pocket.

I stood there in front of everyone, gathering my thoughts.

"He died saving me and taking rounds that ate him from the inside out, for me." I swallowed hard, gritting my teeth. "Whatever he did, however you feel about him, he died fighting alongside us. He found redemption. I hope someday we can find the same."

That was all I trusted myself to say without beginning to mumble or fumble with my words. Angel cried openly. Sam and Preacher had tears running from their eyes. Or rather, Preacher had tears running from one of his eyes.

An awkward silence passed as we all said our last goodbyes to Echo.

"If you guys want to stay, you know you have a home here," I told the remaining members of the Pack. "You always have a home here."

"I've got a lead on Jax on the far side of Mars." Angel wiped her eyes free of the tears. She lifted a hand to stop us before any of us could offer. "Thanks, but like I said before, I need to do this on my own."

"And I need to get back to my family," Sam said, nodding slightly. "I'm sorry I wasn't there. Maybe if I hadn't left, I could have—"

"Could have what?" Preacher asked in a tone that left no room for debate. "You or Angel could have stopped Echo from sacrificing himself? That was his choice. Unless your powers dictate the ability to take away the freedom of freewill from someone, there was nothing anyone could do. Let's not dwell on that any longer."

"Sound advice," Wesley said, joining us and puffing on his cigar. He looked at Preacher. "What about you, old man? You plan to stay around?"

"I think so," Preacher answered, looking at me for direction. "The Pack as we know it is going their own separate ways, but maybe Earth needs its own force to protect it. Maybe the Pack evolves to protect Earth from threats both internal and from the outside universe."

"I like the sound of that," Cryx said, also joining us.

Butch trotted alongside her, tongue lolling out the side of her mouth.

"Does everyone know that I'm going to Earth?" I asked incredulously. "How fast does news travel these days?"

"Hard to keep secrets," X said inside of my head. "But you didn't tell me not to tell anyone."

I turned from the group to talk to X as they went on about plans and saying their own goodbyes.

"You told Preacher and Cryx about Earth?" I asked.

"Let's just be honest with each other for a second, real talk," X answered. "You're not the best with coordinating or communicating with various parties."

"Point taken," I said, this time hearing Cassie come up beside me.

"You doing okay?"

"Define 'okay'?" I asked.

"Emotionally stable? Are you at peace with Echo?"

"Yeah," I said, taking my time to think about her question and give her an honest answer. "I'm at peace with it."

"Good," Cassie said, looking over her shoulder at the others. "I'm not sure what resources you have at your disposal, but if you needed some dropships to help take your things to Earth—why are you smiling at me like that?"

"Oh, just because I'm about to blow your mind," I told her. "X, can you show her the schematics for the thrusters under Dragon Hold?"

# TWENTY-SEVEN

"THIS IS BEYOND INSANE," Preacher said to my right. "I just want to go on record that this is a bad idea."

"Didn't know you were so squeamish when it came to space travel," Cassie said with an arched eyebrow.

"This isn't space travel; this is—this is home travel in space," Preacher answered. "Bapz, are you sure the force field around the manor will hold?"

"Sure—ish," Bapz said with a steel smile. "It's never been really tested. All the run-throughs looked good. Well, if I'm being honest, there was one that—"

"Nope, nope, let's not be honest," I interrupted, sitting in the commander's chair. "Let's just go with 'all is good.'"

Bapz gave me a thumbs-up.

One of the rooms on the top floor of the manor wasn't a room at all. It faced the entrance to the grounds and was a command station. There was an honest-to-crip command station on the top floor of the manor.

It was in a room I had passed dozens of times before on the way to my own chamber. A simple brown door closed off like any other. Once the door was open, however, it was unlike anything I had ever seen.

Holographic monitors at command stations opened to the right and left. A step down, there was the command seat for a captain to direct his crew. A step below that on a lower level held a pair of chairs for the pilot and copilot. The wall facing the outside of the building held a pair of windows that actually opened to reveal a screen.

Right now, our crew consisted of Bapz at the helm with Cassie backing him up. Preacher and Cryx stood behind me at the weapons and shield stations more for support and to see how this was all going to work than to actually man the stations.

Butch sat beside me giving out large brown puppy-dog eyes that said, "Are you crazy enough to actually attempt this?"

"Yes, I am crazy enough," I said to the wolf, ruffling her soft velvet-like ears.

"What did you say?" Cassie asked.

"Nothing," I answered. "Butch is just judging me. Are we ready to do this, Bapz?"

"All systems are green and thrusters are ready to disengage from the planet's crust."

"Well, here we go," I muttered, blowing out a long breath of air. I sank deep into the high-backed captain's seat. On either side of the armrest, there were controls, but I had no idea what they did. "What do we always say, Cryx?"

"Screw the consequences?" she responded.

"What? No." I looked around the seat at her with a grin. "Can't kill our spirit. Here we go. Mr. Bapz."

"Yes, Captain," Bapz shouted, turning back to the controls in front of him. His metal fingers raced across his holographic keyboard. "Fire the thrusters and disengage from Mars."

Cassie sat beside him, her eyes tracking his movements. Bapz noticed and slowed down a bit going over instructions and details of the ship with her, so she could take over if the situation called for it.

Everyone in Dragon Hold who opted to stay and go to Earth inside the manor was buckled in tight throughout the building. They had already been warned and were no doubt as nervous as I was. Our army consisted of Way settlers and former Immortal Corp employees. It was an interesting mix to say the least.

Dragon Hold shuddered and shook underneath our feet. A heavy tremor rolled through the entire building. I felt it first in my feet then through my seat, all the way through my hands and head.

"Switching view to the area around the outer fences," Bapz called, looking up at the giant screen in front of us that now showed an image of the grounds around the outer walls of the property tearing free from the ground.

Sand was tossed into the air as rock was hewn in two. The manor lifted first one then two, then three meters from the ground.

My eyes were seeing it, but my brain couldn't comprehend what was actually going on. Sand at the edge of our ship spilled down to stay on Mars as the rest of the grounds lifted.

For the first time, I got to see the thrusters lifting the manor into the air. Four massive engines spaced out at the four corners of the property, held us aloft. The thrusters themselves looked like massive metal circles shooting fire from the bottom of the manor.

"Is it supposed to be shaking like this?" a white-knuckled Preacher shouted from behind me.

"No idea!" I yelled. "X?"

"Systems are stable," X answered. "Thrusters are operating as they should. Engaging dome."

A second later, a bluish-green dome began spreading from the ground up to create a perfect dome around the manor and grounds.

"This is banana-level stuff right here," Cryx said, shaking her head. "I can't even right now."

The manor lifted higher and higher into the air.

Bapz and X exchanged information and numbers and levels of velocity while Cassie asked questions and learned as much about piloting the craft as she could.

I probably should have been paying more attention to what was going on, but the little kid in me couldn't believe what I was seeing. We were about to enter space, then it was a one-way trip to Earth.

An explosion from somewhere outside disrupted my view of the grounds so far below. One second, I was amazed at how small the Martian city below was becoming, the next, the manor shuddered. We lost altitude for a moment before leveling out, then dropped again.

My stomach felt weightless as we fought to stay in the air.

"Sweet mother of crip!" Preacher exclaimed from his seat. "What's happening!?"

"We've lost power in thruster three," Bapz said, bringing a view of a smoking thruster to the screen in front of us. "I'm checking it now."

We lost more and more altitude as the three remaining thrusters fought to keep us in the air.

Butch whined next to me, getting low to the ground.

The Martian city of Athens below us that once seemed so small was getting larger and larger by the second.

"Come on, come on, come on," Cassie chanted,

opening her own holographic screen to see if there was anything she could do to help with her limited experience.

"I got it, I got it. Give me a second," Bapz yelled.

"We don't have a second," I said as we lost all sense of staying in the air and began to plummet to the ground below us. "We have no time. Let's go, Bapz!"

"I have to restart the engine on thruster three," Bapz called back.

I gritted my teeth as the mansion began to spiral out of control. Now not only were we falling back to Mars, we were spinning in the process.

I'd gotten over my space sickness in a hurry, but right now, it was coming back with a vengeance. I gripped my seat arms tightly. I watched out the front screen as we spun to our death.

The ground was a few meters away and closing quickly when the mansion stopped spinning and shook so hard, I thought the building might come down altogether.

Quick breaths came in and out of my chest more like pants from Butch than normal breathing of any kind.

"Thruster three is back online," Bapz said triumphantly as we hovered in the air right over a neighborhood in Athens.

Our screen showed us an image of an older woman in a robe with curlers in her hair. She had stepped onto her porch to see what was making all the noise.

Her mouth opened so large, I thought her jaw was going to hit her chest. All around the neighborhood, more and more people were coming out to witness the floating mansion above their roofs.

"Hey, maybe we should get out of here before the Galactic Government shows up," Cassie suggested. "Did anyone clear this little trip with them?"

"I sent a note to Colonel Strife, but still, I don't want to have to re-explain myself to the local authorities," X told her. "We should go. I'm already picking up chatter on the comm line about GG units on the way."

"Mr. Bapz," I said once more. "Get us out of here. And is that going to happen again? I mean, the whole almost dropping to our deaths? I just want to be prepared."

"No, no, no," Bapz said with a shake of his metal head. "I fixed the issue. It was a one-time ordeal."

"Good," Preacher said. "My gut can't take much more of that."

I looked back at him and Cryx. Preacher looked like I felt, ready to give up breakfast at a moment's notice. Cryx, on the other hand, was all wide smiles. When she saw me looking, she said, "Let's do it again. That was fun."

"You've got issues, kid," I said with a smile so she'd know I was teasing.

Without any other near death experiences, the manor was in the air once more and soon we were past the Martian atmosphere and traveling into space.

Our next test came when Bapz engaged the hyperspace drive. Traveling through hyperspace looked like a rainbow of colors splashing across our screen. It was beautiful and awe-inspiring at once.

The colors blended together then separated time and time again. There were the richest blues, darkest greens, and most vibrant purples I had ever seen. It was almost mesmerizing if you let yourself get lost in it.

"Did you hear about that GG vessel that entered hyperspace and never came out?" Cassie asked over her shoulder from her seat at the front next to Bapz. "It was a battle class cruiser."

"I heard the reports," Preacher replied. "But I thought it was just a made-up story."

"We have it on good authority that it actually happened," Cassie answered. "At least, that's what the Intel the Order got says."

"What happened?" Cryx asked. "I mean, what happened to the GG cruiser?"

"Hyperspace has a hypnotizing effect on travelers if you allow it," Cassie explained. "There have been a few reports outside of what happened to that cruiser of the same. Other times, the ships simply enter hyperspace and never come out. That's what they think happened to the bridge of the battle class cruiser. They were hypnotized by what they saw in hyperspace and just kept going."

"Wouldn't the rest of the crew try and stop them?" I wondered. "I mean, if it wasn't an entire ship and only the bridge was hypnotized."

"Maybe they locked the bridge, maybe the whole crew did get hypnotized somehow." Cassie shrugged. "I don't think we'll ever know. The name of the ship was the *Reckoner*."

"Well, that horrifying story makes me not want to look at all the pretty colors anymore," I said, getting up from my seat. "We should take shifts two at a time. Bapz, are you okay at the helm? I mean, can you even get hypnotized?"

"Excellent question and no," Bapz said with a thumbs-up. "I'm unhypnotizable, although I'm not sure that's a word. I'm not wired like humans are and not capable of losing myself to the hyperspace lull as such."

"Good to know," I said. "Well, if I'm not needed, I think I'm going to catch some shut eye. When we get to Earth, I'm sure there'll be a lot of work to tackle."

"Are we setting the manor down at the previously discussed location?" Bapz asked as all eyes turned to me. "Oh, didn't you tell anyone else?"

"I'm going to now," I said, addressing the bridge. "I thought we'd stay close to the Phoenix base as well as Sam and her family in the Badlands. I picked a place for us on the western coast of what used to be the United

States. It's close to the Reapers as well and only a four-hour drive to New Vegas if we needed GG support there. It's a place I've been to before so it was all I know. If anyone else has a better idea, I'm all ears."

Out of the group on the bridge, I could guess only Preacher and Cassie had been to Earth before. I assumed Bapz spent his time on Mars and Cryx hadn't mentioned ever going to Earth before.

The bridge remained silent.

"Okay then, I'm going to get some food and sleep. I'll see you all when we reach Earth."

# TWENTY-EIGHT

WHEN WE ENTERED Earth's atmosphere, I was once again seated in my command chair on the bridge. Earth was much of what I remembered my first time there. Bare, desolate, like some kind of skeleton long since laid to rest.

If Phoenix and the Wardens could deliver, then that was all about to change.

Dragon Hold slowly traveled over the western coast where dirty brown water that acted as an ocean where nothing lived lapped onto the shore. Past the mountain range where the Phoenix base code named The Vault sat was a line of steep cliffs that fell off suddenly to the sand then ocean beyond.

"What about on one of those cliff ranges?" X suggested to the bridge. "It'll be defensible and close to both Phoenix and the Badlands."

"I like it," I said slowly. "It looks like home."

"I'll set down there now, but it'll take time to dig the thrusters into the ground," Bapz informed us. "We'll have to sit on them for a while."

"Good by me," I answered.

"Wow," Cryx said from her seat behind me. "I've never seen the ocean before."

We all took a moment to take in the large body of water lapping on the shore. It was hard to believe we were here again. I had gone from the moon to Earth and Mars and back. Now we were on Earth once more, not to fight back an alien invasion but to do something much more difficult.

Somehow, it seemed right to be doing this work after so much death and killing marred my past.

"Setting down," Cassie said, taking the controls.

Bapz looked at her with a raised eyebrow. "Are you sure you're ready for that? Not just anyone can come in and fly the Hold. You need extensive training and—"

"Taking the controls from you now," Cassie continued, punching a few buttons on her holographic desk and screen. "I've been paying attention, Bapz. Don't worry; a girl can learn a few tricks."

Bapz stared wide-mouthed as Cassie took controls from him and maneuvered the Hold to Earth.

"How did you do that?" Bapz asked, amazed. "I had no idea the controls could even be taken from the pilot's seat to the copilot's like that."

Cassie winked at him.

That made me smile again. It seemed I had more reason to do so in the last few days.

Cassie maneuvered the Hold down to the ground like a true professional. It was clear she had extensive piloting skill before boarding the Hold, but still, to maneuver a ship of this kind and size spoke to her skill set.

With a gentle bump, we set down on the cliff. Cassie put the cliff to our rear with the front of the hold facing the barren desert of Earth in front of us.

"Ladies and gentlemen, thank you for flying Dragon Hold Air," Bapz said into a mouthpiece as he addressed the entire ship. "You are now clear to move outside of the Hold and enjoy your new home."

"Cryx, the dome?" X reminded the youngest member of our crew.

"Oh right," Cryx said with a scrunched brow. She turned back to her control panel. She pressed a few buttons X had worked with her on that controlled the shield dome over the Hold.

A moment later, the dome receded back into the ground, allowing access to Earth from the Hold.

"Good work, everyone," I praised, rising from my seat. I knew there was a million and a half things to do now that we were here that included meeting with Phoenix to see how we could help with the planting of the super seeds, talking with Preacher, who volunteered to train a new class of Pack Protocol members, and even getting in touch with Papa to see how we could work with his Reapers.

"Daniel, we have trouble," X said for everyone to hear.

"Of course we do," I replied with a shrug, so used to the idea now, it came as something to be expected. "What is it now? More aliens, mutated creatures on Earth, the Galactic Government decide not to play nice anymore?"

"A large fleet of vehicles coming in from the east," X said. "Bapz, can you bring up a visual?"

"Coming to screen now." Bapz's fingers flew over the keyboard.

The screen transitioned to show dozens of large vehicles eating up the terrain toward us. They ranged from beaten-up transport vehicles to rusted tanks and even what looked like some kind of apocalyptic drop-ship on wheels.

"Can we see what kind of sigil they're flying?" Preacher asked. "It might be Papa and the Reapers."

"No, they're still on Mars helping with the clean-up of the Voy and securing their payment for the help," I supplied. "This is something else, something worse."

I couldn't really tell why, but my hair raised on end. Goosebumps raced down my spine.

"They're flying the Reaper flag, but it's not exactly the same," Bapz said, zooming in on one of the vehicles and the emblem painted on the driver's side door. "It's a Reaper's scythe but different."

We all looked on as Bapz brought the camera to bear on the sigil. He was right. The Reaper sigil was a simple scythe on a green background. This emblem showed a robed figure with a skeleton face and hand holding a scythe.

Bapz zoomed out again to show the level of weaponry the convoy held at their disposal. There were rocket launchers, laser cannons, and other instruments of war that looked like different pieces of weapons hobbled together. The faces of the soldiers in the vehicles didn't exactly scream that they were here to welcome us either.

"I'll go down and see what they want," I said. "Probably a new faction of gangs and tribes that popped up overnight."

"They're too well-equipped," Cassie said, joining me from her seat. "They didn't raise that kind of manpower or vehicles overnight. Not unless they had someone to rally around."

"Daniel," Preacher called as Cassie and I headed for the door. "I'm coming too."

"They'll need you here if anything happens to me," I told him. "You and Wesley watch the Hold while I'm gone."

Preacher looked like he was about to argue.

"Please," I asked him.

"Okay, okay," he said, retaking his seat with Bapz and Cryx. "Remember, we can bring that force field dome up as well. We'll bring the automated defenses online. Just stay close to the entrance so we can light them up if those go bad."

"Will do," I said.

Cassie and Butch fell in step with me as I made my way from the bridge through the Hold.

"For a second, I thought you were going to try to convince me to stay behind," Cassie said without looking at me.

"For a second, I thought about it," I said. "Would it help if I tried?"

"No, I'm going with you no matter what you say," Cassie said as we took the stairs quickly down to the ground level. "Better to save us both some breath."

We exited the manor at the same time, briskly walking over the bridge to the front gates. Through the wrought-iron gates, I could already see the approaching convoy. They were spread out wide, each vehicle shimmering in the hot sun in front of me. A trail of dust kicked up behind each one.

Butch whined as she too sensed the tension of the moment.

I wasn't carrying my knife and axe at the moment, but my MK II hung at my right hip with a fresh drum.

I wasn't too worried about Cassie and her shield, but I was worried about Butch if things got dicey.

"Let's say whoever this is coming wants to fight. I'll heal, but Butch—"

"I'll shield her as best I can," Cassie said. "She'll be fine as soon as she gets in close around them."

"I need to get X and Bapz working on some armor for her soon," I said.

We watched in silence from inside of our own gates as the vehicles arrived at our doorstep. There had to be at least two dozen vehicles parked in front of us and my best guess was over a hundred armed members of whatever gang this was.

Not that I expected to recognize anyone, but unfamiliar dirt-stained faces looked back at me.

Finally, one hulking figure I did recognize stepped from the lead vehicle. He wore dark pants and a vest that showed how massive his arms were. He rivaled Jax for size. A bald head and tattoos covered him much like my own. A scar on the left side of his face completed his look.

Aleron Jacobs stood in front of me with a grin that wasn't at all friendly. There was a promise of violence in his eyes I had come to know well in my own lifetime.

With Dragon Hold still sitting on its thruster instead of the ground, I looked down at him from about a meter above the ground.

"Well, well, well," Aleron shouted through the iron gate. "What do we have here? The same man responsible for fouling up my escape from that GG dropship on the moon all those days ago. Looks like I'm going to be able to pay you back for the favor."

X was like my own personal question and answer forum and I didn't even have to ask the question.

"Aleron broke out of prison a week ago at the same time Papa and the Reapers left for Mars," X read the information to me so fast, her words almost bled into one another. "The GG are hunting him, but as you can see, it looks like a lot of rival gangs have run to his banner."

"No words, huh?" Aleron said with a stare so cold, it would have made most men shudder.

Lucky for me, I wasn't most men.

"Aleron, Aleron, is that you? I thought you were in a hole in New Vegas?" I said with a warm grin as if I meant every word. "And now look at you. Come here to welcome us to our new home and with all your friends present too. How nice. I would have had something ready on the table if I knew you all were on the way. A big strong boy like you looks like he could use a good meal."

All mirth evaporated from Aleron's face.

"You think you can steal the Reapers from me, set up Papa to be their new leader, then come in on my territory and open shop?" Aleron growled. The muscles in his thick neck bulged. "I'm going to tear your eyeballs from their sockets."

"That's disgusting," I said. "Trust me, I've taken a

few eyeballs in my day. It's not what you think. Plus, if you're going to come at us like this, you're going to need to bring a lot more soldiers with you."

"Grimm Reapers!" Aleron bellowed.

At once, every weapon, both handheld and mounted, were pointed at Butch, Cassie, and me.

Butch tossed her head back and bellowed such a howl, I felt the noise reverberate in my chest. I had to fight the urge to cover my ears as the alpha wolf rang a cry so dominating, I almost bowed to her.

Other howls joined hers, first far and then closer and closer. Dragon Hold carried everything inside the gates with us. That included the grounds.

Galloping could be heard behind us as Butch continued her rallying call. Soon, dozens of wolves nearly as large as Butch surrounded us. Brown, black, white, and grey beasts found us and then directed their aggression at Aleron and his Grimm Reapers.

"You think I'm afraid of some little science experiment?" Aleron snarled. "What did you do? Mate wolves with horses? As long as they bleed, I can kill them."

"Kill this," Cassie said, lifting her right hand into the air. "Preacher!"

Mechanical sounds joined the pack of restless howling wolves that paced back and forth on our side of the gate. Automated turrets opened from the ground on our side of the gate. They reached first up then over our wall at the Reapers.

Four of the large weapons with rotating barrels covered the Reapers. While Aleron was brutal, it seemed he wasn't stupid.

"This isn't over," Aleron said through gritted teeth. "You tell Papa when he gets back, he's a dead man. This territory is mine. He was always my number two, but now he won't even live to be that. And don't think I'm not coming for you too."

"You know where I live," I told him without flinching.

Aleron spat up at the gates, then turned to walk away. He boarded his vehicle and they took off in a roar of engines and dust.

"Well, that went well," Cassie said.

"Nice touch, both of you," I said, taking a knee and scratching the bottom of Butch's neck. "Having the wolves come and then the turrets? Very cool."

"We do what we can," Cassie said, looking at the retreating Grimm Reapers. "What do we do about them?"

"Not much we can do," I answered. "We wait, work, and live. We'll be ready once they make their move."

## EPILOGUE

"THE SUN LOOKS SO MUCH different here on Earth," Cassie said as she sipped her glass of water. "I mean, I've seen it plenty of times, but I think it's prettier somehow here instead of on the moon or Mars, like this is how it was always meant to be viewed by humans."

I followed her gaze. She wasn't wrong. The sun painted the sky in a series of rose pinks and purples. It was as if an expert painter had spent the day preparing the sky for this very moment.

We sat on a small flat section of the roof of Dragon Hold. I had Bapz bring us a table, chairs, and meal. He had discovered what Cassie liked to eat through conversation upon my request and it was there now for us. A feast of printed vegetables, meats, and cheeses.

I had to go all out for our first date. I didn't really

know what I was supposed to do, but dinner and a holo film from a projector on the roof during sunset sounded nice in my head.

"I think the sun will be seen by a lot more people here on Earth if we can clean it up," I answered. "I know it'll be a long road, but Phoenix is committed and so are we."

"Still haven't decided on a name for the new corporation?" Cassie asked, popping a piece of printed broccoli in her mouth.

"Not yet. Nothing seems to be just right." I shrugged. "It'll come in time."

"Just like Aleron and his Grimm Reapers?" Cassie asked.

"I warned Papa what was going on here, that his territory was taken over," I said. "Papa's always been easygoing and good-natured, but he seemed scared when I brought up Aleron's name. I'm not sure if he's ready for an all-out war with Aleron or if he thinks he might be better off staying on Mars."

"Either way, Aleron has to be dealt with," Cassie said, wincing as if her head hurt. "Sorry, I always do this."

"Do what?" I asked.

"Start talking shop when we're supposed to be having fun on our date."

"It's okay."

"No, no, it's not," she said, shaking her head. Her

dark hair waved with the motion. I had never seen her in a dress, and to be honest, I had a hard time keeping my eyes off her. She was gorgeous. "You spent all this time setting up this amazing date for us and I'm talking about Grimm Reapers."

"What do you want to talk about?" I asked. A rogue thought popped into my mind. "Hey, when's the last time you were on a date?"

Cassie's eyes widened. Then she reddened. The Cyber Hunter who could throw a man through a wall actually blushed.

"You don't have to answer if you don't want to, but I have to be honest. I kind of want to know more now," I said, wiping my mouth with a clean linen napkin.

"It had to be before joining the Order." Cassie looked into the sky as if she could read the answer there. She squinted with one eye in thought. "I think ten, no, fifteen years ago."

"Wow, well, if it makes you feel any better, this is my first one," I said, putting her at ease. "At least the first one I can remember."

"What?" Cassie said, her eyebrows shooting up to her hairline.

"Yeah, remember the whole memory loss thing?" I asked, pointing to my head. "I know I must have been on them before, but the details are lost to me."

"Well, Daniel Hunt," Cassie said, rising from her seat as she pressed a few buttons on her left forearm. A low, slow tune filled the still air around us. "Most girls like dancing, and if this is the only proper date you've ever been on, I think we need to do you justice."

She came to me, extending a hand.

I took it with hesitation. Not that I was afraid of her. Never her. But that I would fall over my own feet. I wasn't exactly the dancing type. But heck, I could weave my way in and out of a fight pretty well, so how much different could it be?

The sounds of music almost did the dancing for us as we twirled and laughed like we didn't have a care in the world and for the time being that was true. Everything that weighed on my shoulders for the last few days receded like the night in light of the morning sun.

Cassie was beautiful both outside and inside. The better I got to know her, the more I realized she was so much more than a Cyber Hunter. That was a mask she wore around people she didn't know.

The side of her I saw now was like a breath of fresh air in the middle of some kind of toxic fume our galaxy had become.

We danced to a few songs then finished eating and finally sat down on some blankets and pillows Bapz had provided to watch our holo film.

The canopy of stars opened overhead to light our show for us. There were seemingly millions of them twinkling just for us. Without hesitation, Cassie placed her head on my shoulder halfway through the film.

When the film was over, I knew I had to say something. The night had gone too perfectly not to let her know what she was beginning to mean to me. I'd lost too many friends and seen too much death to let fear hold my tongue now. She needed to know and I needed to tell her.

"Cassie," I said to the black hair on my shoulder. She smelled soft and strong in the breeze like some kind of sweet spice. "Cassie, I don't know what's going to happen to us. But I want you to know that I care about you more than just a friend. I'm not trying to freak you out or anything, but I'm so glad our paths crossed, even if we met while you were trying to kill me in the Phoenix Vault. I want more of whatever we have found with each other."

Cassie was quiet. From my vantage point, I could only look down at her hair on my shoulder.

"Cassie?" I asked a little louder. "Are you asleep?"

She was.

I carefully maneuvered her head down to a pillow and looked at how peaceful she was for a moment. I knew then nothing would happen to her. Not that she needed me to take care of her, but still I'd be by her side until I ceased to breathe.

X and I had agreed the AI would remain offline until she heard her name, giving me privacy for the night.

"Hey, X," I said, still looking at Cassie.

"Yes, Daniel?" X responded. "Oh, oh my, did you two—"

"She's sleeping," I said quickly before the conversation could go sideways. "We had a great night. She's just sleeping now."

"Oh, okay good," X said with a heavy breath. Her voice changed from calm to panicked in the space of the next second. All I heard was, "Daniel! Incom—"

All sound except the turrets around the fence line were blocked out as the automated defenses around Dragon Hold came alive. The turrets filled the air around us with the sound of waking thunder.

Bright flashes streaked across the sky. By the time I realized what the turrets were shooting at, it was too late. A ball of black energy struck the top of the roof so hard, it sent a shockwave through me and a rousing Cassie.

I saw the form of the man inside the dark ball before I was blown off my feet and, along with Cassie, sent tumbling down the edge of the slanted roof to what could be our demise floors below.

I didn't think to bring weapons. Still, I tried to grab on to anything I could. The tiles on the roof were too slick. I saw Cassie tumbling beside me. My heart pounded out of my chest. Everything was happening so quickly.

Something like knives being unsheathed reached my ears followed by a tearing sound. Cassie had stopped her fall by using the twin claws on her left forearm, digging them into the roof. With her right hand, she grabbed me and stopped my own fall.

The turrets had stopped firing, unable to get a clean shot at our enemy on the roof.

"Best sleep of my life and woken by an attack," Cassie said to me, swinging me up with her super-human power. I finally got a grip on the roof tiles. "Who's our visitor?"

"I don't know," I said, gripping on to the roof tiles with my fingers and the toes of my boots. "But I'm pissed."

Together, we climbed back onto the short section of the roof.

Over the edge, the man known as Nemesis stood there with a ball of black energy crackling around him. I had the same feeling I did when I saw him before. I knew him somehow. He looked like an older version of myself.

"Daniel Hunt, Cassie Evans, if you want to live, if the future is to survive at all, you have to listen to me," Nemesis told us.

"Who are you?" Cassie asked. She had already brought both blasters on her forearms to bear on the intruder. "If YOU want to live, tell me that now or I swear to all that is holy, I'll kill you."

Nemesis looked at us both with nothing but

honesty in his eyes. "I am the offspring of Daniel Hunt and Cassie Evans."

DANIEL HUNT WILL BE BACK in the next *Forsaken Mercenary* book, *Nemesis*. Grab it now in ebook, paperback and audio HERE or by visiting Amazon.com.

## STAY INFORMED

Get A Free Book by visiting Jonathan Yanez' website. You can email me at jonathan.alan.yanez@gmail.com or find me on Amazon, and Instagram (@author_jonathan_yanez). I also created a special Facebook group called "Jonathan's Reading Wolves" specifically for readers, where I show new cover art, do giveaways, and run contests. Please check it out and join whenever you get the chance!

For updates about new releases, as well as exclusive promotions, visit my website and sign up for the VIP mailing list. Head there now to receive free stories.

*www.jonathan-yanez.com*

Enjoying the series? Help others discover *Forsaken Mercenary* by sharing with a friend.

# BOOKS IN THE FORSAKEN MERCENARY UNIVERSE